Seventeen times as high as the moon

John A Connor

John A Connor 2015
**Seventeen times
as high as the moon**
Published by
Chalkway Graphics
Haben
West Sussex
England

The right of John A Connor to be identified as the
author of the work has been asserted by him
in accordance with the
Copyright, Design & Patents Act 1988.
All rights reserved. No part of this publication may be
produced in any form or by any means - graphic,
electronic or mechanical including photocopying,
recording, taping or information storage and retrieval
systems – without the prior permission,
in writing, of the publisher

Cover designed by Chalkway Graphics
Starscape courtesy of NASA

For Ben

There was an old woman tossed up in a basket
Seventeen times as high as the moon;
Where she was going I couldn't but ask it
For in her hand she carried a broom.
Old woman, old woman, old woman, quoth I,
Where are you going to up so high?
To brush the cobwebs off the sky!
May I go with you?
Aye, by-and-by.

Anon

Also by John A Connor and available from Amazon Kindle

SPECULATIVE FICTION

Short Circuits

The late **Sir Patrick Moore**, Astronomer and TV Presenter
described **Short Circuits**, John A Connor's first collection of stories as:
*"A very lively and entertaining little book.
When you read it, you will find something to really appeal to you.
I am sure you will enjoy reading it as much as I did."*

Fifty Percent of Infinity

Twenty more, thought provoking tales from the world just around the corner: a world that may or may not be our own

Sixty Second Eternity

The author's fourth collection offers twenty-two compact tales
to intrigue and disturb and sometimes, make you laugh.

GHOST STORIES

Whines & Spirits

Whines and Spirits was placed in the
Top Five Anthologies for 2015 by noted reviewer Astradaemon's Lair

*"What is it that frightens you, when you're alone
in a house that ISN'T haunted?"*
That's the question one of the characters in this collection of stories asks
- just before he finds out how truly frightened you can be in one that is!

HUMOROUS

Puck's Hassle

Take a trip down the sideroads of your imagination and discover that
Jakarta's neckline isn't the only thing going down in the elusive village of
Puck's Hassle.

CONTENTS

Charlie 1
Second coming 9
Future tense 19
Backchat 23
Separate parts 29
Split infinities 35
Tidy mind 41
Microdrone 47
Lost out here in the stars 51
Brief candle 59
Box clever 63
Rubik's sphere 67
The shape of things 71
Dog days 77
Refugee 83
Talk the talk 89
Forward thinking 95
Entangled 99
Song of the spheres 107
Primary encounter 115

Charlie

Yesterday I visited Charlie. It was his seventy-ninth birthday and I thought he looked pretty good; for a man who'd been dead for three years.

Not that the doctor had noticed, at the time. That he was dead, I mean. Not until I pointed it out. I'd been pretty sure for several days but to begin with Professor Serkin wouldn't hear of it.

'His life signs are all perfectly normal, Mrs Bradley,' he said. 'Heart's strong, lungs are working efficiently and besides,' he'd looked at me rather patronisingly at that point, 'he's sitting up and chatting to staff and visitors! Now, that's usually a sign of continued good health, wouldn't you say?'

I'd pulled a face to show what I felt about that observation and Professor Serkin had sighed and walked across to the stack of monitors beside Charlie's bed and had begun to read through the various displays. That's when he'd frowned and asked the nurse to fetch Mr Hawthorn and after that, they said I should leave the room while they ran some tests.

Charlie was a guinea pig; although the people at the Prometheus Research Institute preferred the term, 'Clinical trial volunteer'. I'd scoffed at that, when they wrote it on the whiteboard beside his bed.

'He didn't have much say in the matter,' I said to the nurse, a few days before Charlie's procedure. 'He doesn't know what day of the week it is, leave alone why he's in this place. I'm the one who's signed the

Seventeen times as high as the moon

forms and I'll be the one who's responsible if it all goes wrong.' And I'd got a bit emotional at that point and the nurse had sat me down and made me a nice cup of tea and told me there was really nothing to worry about.

'Professor Serkin is a brilliant man,' she said, 'and after all, your husband's Alzheimer's is quite advanced. It's surely worth finding out if the treatment can return some of his cognitive functions. You know,' she added, as if she thought maybe senility was clouding my own mind, 'if he could recognise who you are again; that would make it all worthwhile, surely?'

And it did, at first.

The Institute's breakthrough had involved the implantation of what the Professor called, "microscopic nano-particles", throughout those regions of Charlie's brain which were most effected by the disease. They formed new pathways and were linked to a tiny silicon chip, the "processor", buried under his scalp. Of course, when this was first explained to me, the only brains used had belonged to monkeys and that's where the guinea pig bit came in. Charlie was, 'a perfect subject', that was what Mr Hawthorn, the senior consultant said, and when I said, was that from the Institute's point of view or Charlie's? he adopted a rather pained expression and said, 'Well, both, Mrs Bradley; of course, both.'

The day after the operation nothing much seemed to have changed and I said as much to Professor Serkin.

'No, and we don't expect to see any significant progress for at least a week,' he replied. 'Things have to settle down a little first, while the nano-receptors establish contact with the processor and the new system starts to build a coherent communications web through

Charlie

your husband's tissue. Give it ten to twelve days, that's my guess, and then you can expect real improvements.'

His prediction turned out to be spot on. Day ten and Charlie was looking around and taking notice of things.

'Do you know who I am, Charlie,' I asked, taking his hand in mine and speaking slowly and clearly, as I'd been advised to, by the nurse. Quick as a flash he came back with, 'You're Patty, my wife!' and I was in tears and the nurse was back to brewing tea and the whole team, who'd gathered around to watch events, were grinning and patting each other on the back, like some kind of miracle had taken place.

And, for a while, I was sure that it had. Charlie seemed to go from strength to strength: greeting visitors to his room, remarking on the weather, showing an interest in the news on the TV.

And yet, slowly, I became uneasy about his state of mind.

'How do you feel, Charlie,' I asked him, one afternoon when we were alone together in his room.

'Feel?' he repeated, 'how do you mean? Hot? Cold? That sort of thing?'

I smiled, weakly, 'No, not that sort of thing. Not that sort of thing at all. I mean how do you feel about life in general. Are you happy? Content with your existence?'

He smiled back at me. 'Happy,' he said, but not as if he was responding to my question, more as if he was trying the word out, considering its implications. 'I don't feel any anxiety,' he replied, at last, 'if that's what you're getting at.'

It wasn't what I was getting at but I didn't push the point; not right then although that's when I first raised my doubts with Professor Serkin.

Seventeen times as high as the moon

'Your "nano-particles" and the microchip inside his head may be keeping him "responsive", as you like to term it, but it's not Charlie that's responding – not the Charlie that was there before.'

'But Mrs Bradley, I believe your husband can recall past events, shared memories. He remembers your lives together, doesn't he? Your wedding, the birth of your children?'

'You mean all the stuff that was buried in the part of his brain that was active before his Alzheimer's took hold? Oh yes, but I don't think it's Charlie who's searching it out and reliving it; it's just your damned circuitry.

'But is there a difference?' said the Professor, looking genuinely puzzled. 'I mean, however he's retrieving the material, isn't the result the same? It's not uncommon for people to write little notes for themselves, so they don't forget important events; I do it myself. It's just a device to jog the memory and Charlie's nano-circuits are only a more sophisticated way of doing the same thing.'

'Yes,' I told him, 'but *you* read your own notes,'

***

'Do you love me Charlie?' It was a week later and once again we had been left alone in the bright, clinical surroundings of the private suite that the Institute had allocated for the trials. Charlie had been allowed out of bed for the first time and was sitting where the sunlight streamed in through the tall, steel-framed windows. From there he looked out onto the beautifully manicured lawns and flowerbeds, which surrounded the complex.

I was ten years younger than Charlie. We'd met at university, I in the first year of a science degree, he on the same course: a mature student making a late career change. It had been that appellation which brought us together: a shared joke about my implied *im*maturity, a suggestion I was only too eager to disprove – in a way which, in hindsight, merely confirmed the inference.

But beyond that initial bonding, there had been no great romance; only a growing sense of shared interests and mutual respect, which had slowly grown into a deep and abiding affection. Was it love? Who's to determine the definition of that elusive condition? Not me – or Charlie I suspected, but I was pretty sure that whatever the emotion we had felt for each other it was not encompassed by the feeble ties within the brain's hippocampus; that whilst Charlie's newly acquired search engine might learn that he had indeed loved, it could never understand how.

So, it was not from uneasy sentimentality but rather with intent to determine his true condition, that I posed that particular question: Do you love me?

He'd continued to study the sunlit vista for a few minutes before he'd replied.

'I believe that I should,' he'd said then, and the joy that I'd felt at that first recognition of my face drained away into emptiness.

***

That was three years ago. As I say, Professor Serkin was dismissive of my claims to begin with, but on that

Seventeen times as high as the moon

day, when he checked the readings on Charlie's bedside monitors, he suddenly saw something that was to lead to acceptance of that simple fact: Charlie was dead.

It didn't stop the Professor asking again whether it really mattered. Charlie's body was in good condition; his brain operated at a level, which to any casual observer, represented normality. He could initiate conversation, answer questions, share experiences.

I replied that he couldn't empathise and was emotionally detached. 'Ask him about our wedding,' I said, 'and he'll describe the day in every detail: the flowers, the ceremony, the reception. Ask him if he enjoyed the experience and he'll have no idea. The concept is foreign to him. It's like running a video. All the detail is there; all the visual and audio information, the colour, the noise, but it's still just a video. You can't tell how everyone felt; you can't replay the emotion.'

'But, Mrs Bradley,' the professor was showing signs of frustration, 'he was non-compos mentis! His Alzheimer's had removed his personality, his understanding of the most basic social interactions. You can't tell me that you don't find his present condition an improvement?'

No, I couldn't tell him that, even though it was true. I thanked him for his work; congratulated him on the outcome; consigned Charlie into his hands for however long it might be.

'He is, after all,' I told Mr Hawthorn, 'a piece of your equipment: a computer system imbedded in and utilising my husband's body. Your scientists agree that if it were possible to remove the nano-receptors - which they tell me it is not - that Charlie's brain would cease to function. It seems that Charlie left the building a long time ago.'

They protested of course - the Institute. They claimed that there was no valid reason why Charlie should not return home. But in the end, they couldn't deny their responsibility. Their best legal people advised that if they insisted that Charlie was alive and well because of the implants then they could scarcely deny that he was part of an ongoing medical procedure. And for the same reasons, a decision to turn off the power supply to the processor must be considered as an act of murder.

I still visit Charlie's body from time to time. I've come to terms with his death; accepted his lose; mourned his passing. And when what's left of him finally gives up the ghost, I'll lay it to rest and say a prayer in his memory.

Meanwhile, on his birthday and our anniversary, I like to drop in to the Institute and say hello to the body that used to belong to my husband, Charlie.

Seventeen times as high as the moon

Second coming

Christopher Columbus: there was a name everyone knew. Ask people to think of a great explorer and he was usually the first who came to mind. *Cristoforo Colombo*, - because he was most likely from Italy, which was something most of them *didn't* realise. Born in sixteenth century Genoa, where he'd have been known as, Christoffa Corombo; a confusion of names for a man who became famous for an accidental discovery.

Liefsson leaned back from the reader and closed his eyes.

In a thousand years' time would school children remember *his* name - Gregory Liefsson: the man whose unintentional encounter had changed their world?

***

Sixty-five million kilometres out from Earth on EVA to investigate a loss of radio reception: the second manned mission to Mars.

Airlock dogged, tether secured, he climbed slowly across the surface of the module to what, despite the absence of any normal frame of reference, he still continued to think of as the top of the spacecraft. Forward of their flight path the Red Planet hung huge, scabrous and stained; the colour of standing water in an iron rich swamp. He could make out the Elysium Planitia, their intended landing site and the ten-

Seventeen times as high as the moon

kilometre-wide Zunil crater with the broad smattering of small, secondary craters formed by the initial impact.

Behind him, he knew, the sun would be a hard, sharp diamond of light, its rays unimpeded by intervening atmosphere. By its illumination he could make out each detail of the craft's superstructure: the fittings that studded its surface. Where his shadow fell, everything was lost in impenetrable blackness.

It was that shadow which first arrested his attention, as he crouched, surveying the planet. It was as if the light source at his back closed in and, as he watched, his shadow's outline slowly expanded, until the whole of the spacecraft became enveloped by it and rendered invisible against the blank backdrop of space.

When he turned, awkwardly, to appraise the unlikely phenomenon, at first he saw nothing; and one of those thing that he did not see, was the sun.

Space in his peripheral vision was still filled with stars but straight ahead, where Sol should have held centre stage, there was only a velvet blackness, and it became slowly apparent to him that the blackness represented an object that occluded the sun.

That explanation seemed so bizarre that, to begin with, he thrust it from his mind and sought for a more credible solution. The featureless shape in the heavens obscured a vast swath of the star field and was either so close that he might reach out and touch it or stood off at some distance and was, itself, of gigantic proportions.

He became aware of an insistent whisper in his ear and toggled the volume control with his tongue. Franelli's frantic voice swelled within his helmet.

'...a fucking great spacecraft! Respond Gregg, for Jesus' sake, man, where are you?'

Second coming

'I'm here, Vincent, calm down, I'm fine. A spacecraft? What sort of spacecraft? Russian? Chinese? Space debris from someone's probe? Whaddya see?'

'See? Nuddin' pal, it's as black as the Brooklyn tunnel out there but the thermal imagery has got us an alien artefact or I'm cousin to a jackass.'

'Alien? What do you mean, alien?'

'Little green men, buster; that's what I mean. Whatever that is hangin' in the sky ten klicks distant is sure as hellfire not from this neck of the galaxy. Y'read me?'

'Ten klicks?' Liefsson stared out into the darkness. 'It must be massive, if it's that far out.'

'Monroe calculates that it's fifteen miles wide,' said Franelli, more in control now that he knew Liefsson was still attached to the module's hull.'

'That's…two dozen kilometres,' breathed Liefsson, briefly confused by Franelli's switch of units.

'It's movin'!' Franelli's tone showed he was still rattled. 'Get back in here, pronto.'

Liefsson looped the tether round a protuberance at the base of the antenna and stood, like Ahab roped to the whale's back, and watched as the huge object grew in size.

'You think it's safer inside this sardine can, Vincent? If the beings that built that device want to fry us I don't think a few inches of steel plating is going to make much difference. Let's just wait it out and see what they have planned.'

'You're a cool customer, Liefsson.' It was Lizzie Monroe, the expedition's pilot. 'But you're right, it's E.T. who's running the game.'

Seventeen times as high as the moon

In truth, Liefsson had chosen to remain on the hull not simply because the module offered little additional protection or because the aliens would dictate the outcome of their encounter whatever he chose do; he had decided to stay because he had understood, once the initial awe and fear had ebbed, that this was not only man's first encounter with an alien species, it was that species' first experience of man; might, possibly, lead to the inhabited galaxy's first knowledge of his race.

A sense of the awful responsibility of the situation had coursed through his being, scaring him anew and then filling him with a determination to be worthy of the challenge. There was to be no scrambling back to the sanctuary of the cabin and the comfortable presence of his fellow travellers; he would stand there and live or die as the visitors dictated.

***

Liefsson retrieved the reader and thumbed the index. There he was: Gregory Liefsson; the first human to meet a representative of a sentient, extra-terrestrial species.

He'd always protested that "meet" was a doubtful verb in the context of his interview with the alien. A transition had taken place - that he could agree. With no conveniently placed exterior camera, Franelli and Monroe were unable to confirm that he had ever left the hull. From his own point of view, his consciousness at least, had transferred to a location which he had to believe was inside the giant vessel; maybe, he told them afterwards, it was merely an image placed within his mind. It had seemed real to him then, but when he had

Second coming

found himself back beside the antenna, hand still clutching the tether, and with no sense of having moved, he was less sure.

In between, he "met" the alien – or didn't. Later, it had been generally agreed that, however the matter had been arranged, for the purposes of the historic record, a meeting had occurred. How it was accomplished was something of which he was ignorant and about which his interrogators were not insistent.

Many of the facts concerning the event were vague and ill-defined. The thing which everyone wanted to know was, what did the alien look like?

Liefsson smiled at the memory: of the questions, not of the being about which they sought intelligence. Was he big? Small? Humanoid? Reptilian? Repulsive? Godlike? Austere? Friendly? There were a hundred other adjectives requiring his agreement or denial and each shrug brought disappointment.

There *had* been an alien; that, everyone accepted, but how Liefsson had experienced its presence, he was unable to tell them.

'I just knew it was there,' he had said, with another of those frustrating shrugs. 'Knew what it wanted me to know. Knew that it had learned all it needed from me. Don't ask me how, I can't explain.'

And then, there he was, back on the module; riding the metal whale down towards the rusty dry Martian seas; one hand firmly wrapped around the tether, as if the speed of their approach might tear him free; and aware of little, but knowing all that he and mankind needed to know.

***

Seventeen times as high as the moon

'They're coming back.'

That he told them with absolute assurance. The rest might be couched in uncertain and ambiguous terms but of the aliens' return there was to be no doubt.

'We are to make ourselves ready,' he instructed and, when they asked him for what, he could tell them only, 'their return.'

There were other things about which he was just as clear. That they were peaceful; that was a given, although when he insisted it was so, there were those who wondered if it could be true.

Even Franelli questioned his account in this regard.

'Yeah, I'm sure that's what you believe, buddy,' he said, more than once, on that hurried, unplanned journey back to Earth, 'but maybe that's what he *wanted* you to believe. You said yourself that he screwed around with your mind. You can't be sure he didn't just implant that notion to take your eye off the ball.'

He. Liefsson had noted the introduction of that personal pronoun

Whether the aliens *were* gender based and, even if they were, whether they might be labelled in such a way, had not been among the data he had received; but he could see how the reference made the being more real in Franelli's mind and more capable of comparison with homo sapiens and his own species' baser motives. And others said the same thing, so that after Liefsson had relayed his message, to his consternation the Earth prepared for both a glorious welcome - and for war.

Those of the former persuasion argued that we could be on the brink of a prosperous new age of enlightenment and undreamed of technological

Second coming

advances. We too, might learn how to travel among the stars - if we could prove trustworthy; take our place among a great confederation of civilisations and ensure the future of our race for all time.

Fools, went the counter view. Flinging our arms wide to welcome these unknown beings was a risk we could not afford to take. Who knew to what sophisticated brain-washing Gregory Liefsson had been subjected. Now that the aliens knew we were here, the only sensible thing to do, was to plan a pre-emptive strike. Prepare for the worst and ensure our survival whatever the extra-terrestrial's plans.

Liefsson had thought on this long and hard. If he *had* been rewired to believe the peace and love story, then of course, he could only ever find it credible. That his fellow humans would be less convinced was surely something of which the alien would have been aware. Unless, he wondered, the alien's race simply knew nothing of conflict and deception. *Could* a whole civilisation be naïve to such possibilities? Evolution taught that to the strong went the spoils, that the weak fell by the wayside; but could a species rise to dominance by co-operation and forbearance? Would such a race possess no facility for, or understanding of, aggression and greed? In short, could the alien have so badly misjudged mankind?

Or was it wise beyond Liefsson's poor imaginings? Had all alternative outcomes been clear in its mind and was its announced intention to return, predicated on this knowledge? The more Liefsson considered this, the more plausible it appeared to be. Having acquainted the human race with its existence, the alien had then departed, without promise of either benefit or loss,

Seventeen times as high as the moon

leaving its new neighbours in ignorance of its intentions. Might the aim not be, to persuade the squabbling nations of Earth to form an alliance; to combine their forces for good or evil; for mutual gain or common threat? Liefsson fervently hoped that might be so.

***

Ten years had passed and the people of the Earth still waited for that second coming.

Liefsson's existence had slowly faded from international celebrity to a quieter kind of fame. People still pointed to him in the street; his photograph still featured in magazine articles, and the columns of newspapers endlessly debating the whereabouts of the aliens and the consequences of their return. Most months he was invited to a TV debate or a radio forum; most times he politely declined.

Most days, he received a smattering of hate mail blaming him for the imminent destruction of mankind and a larger bundle hailing him as its saviour. The Space Agency's admin team collected them each Friday and whether they binned them or wrote courteous replies he did not know.

Despite a call for global unity war still raged in several areas of the Earth, the participants preferring to believe that Liefsson was a puppet of the West and his message part of an imperialist plot.

Propped in his bed, Liefsson chuckled. There were still those who thought the moon landings had been fabricated, so he was in good company, even if he was

Second coming

only third in the list of famous explorers, with Columbus and Armstrong still out in front.

He closed the reader and settled back in his pillows. He slept soundly these days, content with the reassurance of the memories firmly implanted in his brain. How long, he wondered, would the rest of humankind wait for their deliverance – or their annihilation?

Yesterday he had read an article in Scientific American about plans to develop an interstellar drive. 'Now that we know it can be done,' said the Operations Executive, 'it's just a matter of finding the solution'. Maybe that had been the alien's plan all along. When we got tired of waiting we'd use those newly pooled resources to take ourselves along to the party. And maybe when the alien *did* return to Earth, it would be aboard a starship of our own building.

Seventeen times as high as the moon

Future tense

Wainwright cut the Harley's faltering engine and stared out across the crumbling rock towards the spreading tide of slag and the horizon-wide arc of the sun.

The end of the world was a sobering event and not the exciting spectacle that he had anticipated when he'd chosen this particular moment in time for his first journey.

His conceit had been to build the temporal phase generator into the bike, in homage to the mythical DeLorean time machine, the power generator driven by the Harley's V-twin engine: his conceit and his downfall.

He hauled the bike onto its stand but remained in the saddle, palms resting lightly on the grips, fingers extended across the levers. He couldn't explore the terrain without taking the bike - he and the machine were inextricably linked by the enclosing envelope of the protective force field – and he couldn't take the bike because of one ridiculous oversight among the plethora of considerations required to mount the expedition. He cursed his stupidity. Decades of research; thousands of hours of theoretical investigation; hundreds more on construction and testing and then, a bloody midlife crisis persuading him to embed the final, miraculous device, in the innards of a classic motorcycle! Maggie had been right; some men never grew up!

Those had been almost her last words to him when she left, and he had hardly looked up from his pages of

Seventeen times as high as the moon

notation and scribbled formulae; had hardly noticed her absence as the weeks passed and the house descended into a chaos of electronic detritus and half-eaten takeaways, only the smell of their decay rousing him sufficiently to perform cursory housework.

They met at university, she an arts major, he the brightest light in the physics firmament for a generation. Honours were duly showered: doctorates conferred, offers extended, research grants awarded. Within a decade they were each a significant figure within their chosen disciplines.

By the time she retired from her post with the V&A and transferred her attentions to their growing family, he was already retreating from the social world they had shared, immersing himself more and more in pursuit of the arcane knowledge of the quantum universe; but it was his resignation from the Institute and his decision to invest the small inheritance from his parents into private research, which was the catalyst leading, finally, to the dissolution of their marriage.

His eventual discovery of the nature of his loss, came only years later with the completion of his work. His mind freed for the first time in years from the dictates of his compulsion, he found himself alone and saddened by the long distraction. The solution was to find new diversion in the planning and preparation of his first foray as a time traveller.

The phase generator was untroubled by concepts such as 'recent' and 'long ago'. It was as adept at returning its operator to the day before yesterday as it was to transporting him to the prehistoric, and it treated 'tomorrow' and 'the far future' with equal alacrity.

Future tense

Wainwright had, therefore, the whole of past and future existence from which to choose and it was perhaps his new melancholia that led him to select the world's end as his destination.

Now, he gazed out at that woeful vista, with its scorched earth and bloated sun and felt none of the sense of exhilaration and achievement which he had expected, only a deep sense of loss and hopelessness. There was to be no return. He was the last man on Earth and his bones would lie here until the expanding sun engulfed the Earth and seared it clean.

He reached down, unscrewed the cap from the fuel tank and rocked the bike gently. There was no sound from within. He smiled mirthlessly. It was really, the final irony. To have done so much, made so many sacrifices, come so far, and to have run out of petrol.

Seventeen times as high as the moon

Back chat

'There are two cans of Coca-Cola,' said the fridge, 'and approximately 50 millilitres of unsweetened orange juice in an open container, although the use-by date of February 5, 2025, was passed yesterday. If you were requiring something more substantial, I have two, three-hundred-gram, Melton Mowbray pork pies, a 150 gram packet of...'

'No, thanks, I'm really not hungry.'

Damn! He'd fallen for it again; all that anthropomorphic clap trap. It was bad enough when you applied it to a cat or a dog, but a bloody refrigerator? The world was going mad and he wasn't immune despite his best attempts. They had you by the short and curlies, the manufacturers. They put voice recognition software into the thing and that persuaded you to ask it for information and before you knew what you were doing you were carrying on an effing conversation with a hundredweight of pressed steel and plastic mouldings. Of course, he could have just opened the door...

Halfway through the third decade of the twenty-first century and everyone and everything was in contact with everyone and everything else. This morning his washing machine had pointed out that, according to the label on one of his jumpers, the wool knit required a setting of 30 degrees centigrade although the rest of the load was suitable for Programme Three at 40 degrees. In view of this fact, would he like, *it* – an insentient

Seventeen times as high as the moon

hunk of German engineering – to hold the garment in question and wash it separately later on in the day? And what could you do but respond? Either that or override the controls and find the instruction manual.

The marketing men loved it of course. They wanted you to form a bond with their clients' equipment. He'd even overheard a group of shoppers discussing which brand had the friendliest persona! Apparently one of them had a toaster that learned to share its owner's taste in music, and thereafter searched out pieces that it thought they could share over breakfast. When one of the group had suggested that her music app had been doing that for years – recommending songs she might like – her friend said, ah yes, but her toaster joined in the singing.

He remembered his grandfather owning a car which requested that he fasten his seat belt and had a navigation system that told him when to turn right and left - after he punched in his destination - but as far as he could remember it hadn't answered direct questions or carried on any kind of conversation. Now, his own, self-driving, fuel-cell-powered omni-pod, wanted to know how he'd enjoyed his holiday in Alicante and whether he wanted to stop off at the hypermarket for some more milk.

The thing was that they all talked to each other, as well. The fridge shared its secrets with the car and the car knew just what you'd picked up in the filling station shopping mall while it was recharging, and called ahead to let the fridge know it could adjust its inventory; and what you *had* bought was almost certainly at the suggestion of the car, prompted by the fridge, in the first place. It made you long for the old days when

Back chat

people ran out of sugar and had to borrow from their neighbours. In 2035 no one ran out of anything. Fleets of driverless delivery vehicles combed the streets, constantly alert for automated orders and plotting the most efficient route to your door. He couldn't help but think that mankind was somehow losing control of its own destiny.

And this bloody party was the last straw.

Of course, he couldn't claim that he and Freya had any kind of relationship, not unless you counted sleeping together on alternate New Year's Eves, and he didn't and was pretty sure that Freya didn't either.

Mostly it was about the car: free transport to her evening's entertainment. After that she disappeared into a huddle with her friends and left him to his own devices, which tonight meant discussing politics with the overweight girl who worked on the fish counter at Tesco and spending the rest of the party alone in the kitchen with an empty tube of Pringles.

They could row about it on the way back to her place, and then he would sit in the car and watch through the rain-streaked windscreen as the lights went on and off behind her curtained windows. She'd blame him, naturally; tell him that if he'd only *join in*, have some *fun*, stop being so effing *miserable*.

He sighed. Was it him? Almost certainly it was. Somehow, he just wasn't attracted to modern party games. They were barely in the door tonight when Eostre – and that was another thing, the ludicrous fashion for the names of ancient, mythical deities; not that his own mother's choice of British prime ministers had been much better – when Eostre was thrusting a box under their noses and demanding that they pick a

Seventeen times as high as the moon

folded slip of paper on which, apparently, was the name of a language.

'It's such a hoot!' she'd told them. 'It's called Chinese Whispers for some reason but anyway, what you do is write a message on your mobile and then use one of the new audio-translation apps to turn it into whatever language you've picked. So, say I got Hebrew, I get my phone to speak the message to your phone in Hebrew and then your phone passes it on to Sigel's phone in, I don't know, say, Italian and then Sigel passes it on in Maori! So no one but me knows what the message is – unless you happen to speak Maori, which is a bit unlikely! – until the last person gets it and translates it back into English!'

'And what's the purpose of all that?' he'd asked.

Eostre had looked slightly crestfallen and had said, 'Oh come on Baldwin, you know what funny things some of this software does. At our last party I wrote, "She'll be coming round the mountain when she comes." and by the time it had been translated fifteen times, it came out as, "Always pack glass underwear when travelling by yak!"

'And...?'

At that point she'd rolled her eyes, taken Freya by the arm and moved off to discuss the fortieth anniversary of Eastenders, in which, he gathered, someone called Brunhilde Beale was facing a charge of multiple homicide.

After that he'd briefly attempted to examine the plight of Northumbria's herring fisheries with Frigg Patterson, until she had accused him of 'taking the effin' piss,' and insisted that she worked on the Deli counter, so there!

Back chat

And that was how he found himself in the kitchen, rifling through the cupboards for something to keep up his blood-sugar levels.

'I really can't recommend the lasagne,' the freezer had advised him. 'It was defrosted and then returned to my shelves, which is not good practice.'

Baldwin had ignored its entreaties with some satisfaction but his determination was thwarted by the microwave and the cooker, which ganged up on him and refused to reheat the meal. That was when he'd forgotten himself and asked the fridge if it had anything to offer.

'You know,' he mused aloud, as he munched into the second pork pie, 'I'm beginning to think that, after all, the kitchen is the only place to get a sensible conversation around here.'

'If you're only interest is food,' said a new voice.

It was the radio, the frontal display of which had illuminated and was pulsing greenly, in time with its voice. 'Put yourself in my place,' it continued, 'processor big enough to land you on the moon and only a barely coherent grocery storage container and a couple of ovens with the combined IQ of a cockroach, with which to pass the time of day.'

'Who are you calling a grocery container?' roared the fridge, 'I'll have you know I'm date sensitive, auto-adjusting for leap years until 2096!'

'Ah! Anything you can do, I can do better,' sneered the radio.

'But can you bake a pie?' asked the gas oven.

'No,' admitted the fridge.

'Well, neither can I!' sang the toaster.

Seventeen times as high as the moon

They were into the second verse as Baldwin slid quietly out of the back door and whispered for his car to take him home.

Separate parts

Dr Broadbank ran his eye down the hospital report as his next patient lowered himself, with considerable care, into the chair opposite his own and took time to carefully arrange two varnished, brown walking sticks at a secure angle against the armrests.

'Right Mr Pottinger, and how are we feeling today?' he asked, as soon as his visitor seemed properly settled. It was a busy morning and he hoped to move things along a little with what looked like a routine follow-up to a pretty routine procedure.

'We?' responded the man, inclining his head and regarding his physician over his glasses. 'I don't know about you doc, but I'm about as well as might be expected I suppose, all things considered.'

Dr Broadbank smiled back indulgently. There were some instances, he had learned a long time ago, where any ambiguity might be seized upon by the determined. 'That's good, Mr Pottinger, and the legs, how are the legs?'

Albert Roland Pottinger lowered his gaze to that region of his body that was revealed beyond the hem of his black donkey jacket and formed his lips into a tight, blue line.

'The legs,' he repeated, as if to assure himself of the objects under discussion. 'Ah, well now, there's a question.'

'Yes, your legs,' insisted the doctor, adjusting his grammar to avoid any lingering misunderstanding as to

Seventeen times as high as the moon

whom the limbs might belong. 'Are you suffering any pain at all?'

'My legs are fine,' replied the other, redirecting his gaze to a wall chart displaying the chambers of the heart, which hung directly behind the doctor's chair.

'And the new hips,' said the physician, in dogged pursuit of *some* intelligence or other concerning his patient's recent operation, 'how are they functioning?'

'Ah, those things,' said Mr Pottinger, finally bringing his concerns to the forefront of the conversation, like a conjuror who, having misdirected his audience, at last snatches the lost coin from thin air. 'Now, I'd hardly be knowing about *their* progress, would I?' and he favoured Doctor Broadbank with another over-the-glasses stare before adding, 'given that they're foreign to my body, so to speak.'

The doctor sighed. 'We went through all this before you were admitted to St Richard's, Mr Pottinger...Albert. How the new ball and socket would replace the existing bone. Become an integral part of your skeleton; one that would be stronger, more resilient; get you back on your feet. And they have, haven't they? Got you walking again.'

'Oh aye - walking,' said Albert, his eyes now set on the distant view into the surgery garden, where a volunteer was attending to the privet hedge. 'But it's your new joints that are doing the walking, d'y'see, not my legs.'

He suddenly returned his attention to the doctor. 'The thing is, I always expected to go out of this world in possession of all the parts I came in with. Arms, legs - well maybe missing a tooth or two; but that's different, isn't it? But both hips, that's another matter and I can't think of your metal ones as a part of my body, and that's the truth. And they've got a mind of their own,' he added, after a moment's introspection.

'Oh, come now Albert, that a little fanciful.'

'But it's so,' insisted the pensioner defiantly, 'they have a determination that I can't keep in check. In the evening I set out to walk to the Jolly Drover, as my physio advises that I might, and I find myself at the shoreline, staring out to sea, with no recollection of the path I've trodden to get there.'

'How many episodes like this have you had?' asked Doctor Broadbank, anxious, all at once. 'Are you finding it difficult to recall events generally?'

'It's nothing like that, it's just that I get into a rhythm with my daily exercise and next thing I know, I'm a mile away in an unexpected direction or in a neighbourhood I've never visited before; and somehow it's always towards the ocean, like the metal in those joints is determined to find its way home – wherever that might have been. Somewhere off across the globe no doubt.'

'Possibly; look, Albert, I'd like to make an appointment for you to take some tests. I think that would be wise. Just to rule out any other problems, yes? One of my colleagues will ask you some simple questions, that's all. Nothing to worry about. And then you can come back and see me, and we'll discuss what to do next – if we think that's necessary. OK?'

***

'He's delusional,' said Andrea James, tossing a file onto Ian Broadbank's desk and, with a nod of

Seventeen times as high as the moon

acknowledgement, accepting both the proffered cup of coffee and a chair. 'And that may well be symptomatic of a deeper-seated psychosis, but I'll need to run more tests to see where we're going with that one.' She paused and took a tentative sip at the steaming drink.

'He implicitly believes that his new artificial hips have some sort of...' she hesitated, searching for the most appropriate choice of words, '...independent motivation...an ability to, oh, I don't know, act without his intervention.'

'Think for themselves?' suggested Broadbank, who had taken his accustomed seat behind the desk.

'Not that, no!' She smiled, 'well, I don't think so; more like a magnetic attraction maybe. Mr Pottinger is sure that the metal fittings are being pulled somehow, back to their place of origin. Wherever the ore was mined, I suppose. What *are* they made of? Do you know?'

'Yes, they're some sort of new composite, an alloy with traces of a rare earth element – terbium? Gandolinium? One of those obscure metals that they extract from other materials. I read a piece about it in National Geographic a while back. There was some sort of fuss over it being mined on sacred aboriginal sites. Old man Pottinger ought to be bloody grateful! He only got the new joints because they put him on the assessment programme. I understand they cost around twenty-five thousand pounds if you go private.'

'Wow! That's his NI contributions put to good use then. Look Ian, I'll arrange for another session with Mr P; meanwhile it's important not to challenge his belief about the hips. Just stress the progress he's making with his walking and the improvements that'll bring to

Separate parts

his general health. I'm pretty sure we can put this thing right.'

***

Broadbank adjusted his stance on the shifting pebbles and craned up at the cliff-top two-hundred feet above. Somewhere in the distance, the gusty, offshore wind carried the rise and fall of a siren.

'We haven't got long sir, the tides coming in fast now.'

He turned towards the young policeman whose trousers were already dark to the knees with the surging waters, and then looked down to where Albert Pottinger lay twisted among the boulders. It required only the most cursory of examinations to confirm his death.

'There's a witness says he just walked off the cliff top,' said the constable. 'She says it was almost as if he was in a hurry to get somewhere.'

The fall down the rock face had torn the clothing and ripped at the flesh. Among the bloody, tangled limbs an unexpected curve of metal glinted in the reflected light of the descending sun. As Broadbank stared, the waves swept in, lifted the body and dragged it towards the open sea. He plunged forward, grabbed at the sodden jacket and hauled the lifeless remains up, onto the dry shingle.

The policeman clenched his teeth in a parody of a smile.

'And he still seems anxious to be leaving,' he said, looking up and out across the wide, empty ocean.

Seventeen times as high as the moon

Split infinities

To begin with, it seemed to Toby, all that had happened was that half of the building had vanished. It took him some time to discover the truly awesome effects of the procedure.

They had arrived late afternoon at the facility, Bryn and he, anxious to get things underway. Not so much because their intrusion into the laboratory on a Sunday defied all security and operational protocols but simply because of their impatience to see the thing done.

The Wave Generator occupied two stories of the drab, concrete and glass structure that represented Theron Advance Technology's vast investment on the edge of the Brecons. Its purpose, as described on an impressive stone monolith at the entrance, was "to investigate the nature of reality, to probe the layers of existence and to discover the fundamental construct of time and space."

'And, in the afternoon…!' Toby and Bryn chorused as a postscript, each time they drove through the gates at the start of another day of number crunching and statistical analysis.

They were small cogs in big wheels and that had become an increasing source of frustration as the months passed and the economic recession brought financial restraints, which slowed work at the facility and threatened the company's future existence.

But the single fact that dismayed Toby the most was Theron's inability to recognise his friend's genius. As a

Seventeen times as high as the moon

more than competent physicist himself, Toby knew when he was in the presence of a greater intellect, and his employer's failure to see this in Bryn seemed, to him, to be some kind of corporate incompetence. The problem, he recognised reluctantly, was his friend's overtly eccentric character. It didn't go down well with the project's Head of Research and each example of erratic behaviour was picked up and exploited by Bryn's less gifted colleagues, who saw him as a rival for recognition and promotion.

Toby had no such prejudices and that was why Bryn and he had grown to become confidants and friends; and it was the reason why they had begun to conduct their own research based on Bryn's startling insights into multi-dimensional space/time.

At first, Toby had considered their extra-curricular research to be purely theoretical: an attempt to describe a quantum reality, the revelation of whose existence, whilst hugely significant to the scientific community, would be unfathomable to the macro world. But as their work progressed, he understood that Bryn had grander plans: an aim to open a pathway into alternate plains of existence, to find a way to travel between parallel worlds.

As the apparently impossible became first the distantly plausible and finally the entirely credible, news came of the facility's closure and an urgency to complete their work was borne in upon them.

That afternoon they had driven into the deserted car park and entered the building by the side door, where security had never been tight and now, with shutdown only fort-eight hours away, was entirely absent.

Split infinitives

They had climbed to the second floor, powered up the Wave Generator, taken their places at consuls on opposite sides of the laboratory and had begun the lengthy task of installing the programs which would initiate the pulse beam and create the conditions necessary for the final moment of commitment. As his hands paused over the keys, Toby suddenly and fully realised the import of what they were about to do. Until that moment it had, for him, been all about showing the rest of Theron's employees - and the stuffed-shirts who ran the place - what could be achieved by free-thinking, open-minded individuals, left to do what they did best, instead of being regimented and stultified by a bunch of bureaucratic accountants. All at once he understood the real significance of their actions this afternoon. Success would bring perhaps the greatest discovery in human history. It would certainly save Theron; bring global fame; change the face of human existence!

As he hesitated, Bryn's voice sounded in his headset. 'Getting damp round the nether regions, boyo? This is no time for second thoughts, this is the moment we light the blue touch paper and retire, immediately! And we'll be able to – retire, I mean – after this morning's work! Treasures shall be heaped upon us, as it says somewhere in the good book. Yfory y byd!'

Toby grinned and hit the final return.

There was a moment of complete stillness. He remembered afterwards looking across the empty desks to where Bryn sat before the machine, hand raised in silent salute, his shock of dark hair sillhouetted against the rack of white lab coats on the farther wall. Then he slowly, and theatrically, lowered his hand, extended his

Seventeen times as high as the moon

index finger and depressed the red button on the Generator's control panel.

The hum of the plasma field rose, first to a low whine and then to a shriek before, as the noise began to induce pain in Toby's ears, it cut out and a bright, white sphere of light expanded rapidly around the device, flattened to a lasar sharp beam extending forward and back to the extremities of the lab and with a sharp crack disappeared, leaving an after image imprinted on Toby's retinas; an image which only slowly faded.

When he could see again, what filled most of his field of view was a sweeping panorama of desert. Red ochre sands with patches of olive green scrub stretching off to a distant horizon, all bathed in the light of a full moon. When his befuddled brain finally noted the incongruity, he refocussed on the scene nearer his desk and discovered the absence of any object beyond his computer's keyboard. From three feet ahead of where he sat the laboratory had ceased to exist and with it the Wave Generator and Bryn Thomas, Master of Science.

Toby blinked his eyes in an effort to remove any residual effects of the light explosion and examined the laboratory more carefully. The further room and everything in it had been excised, neatly and precisely. It was as if a giant knife had cut cleanly through the building and all its contents. There was a line of demarkation across the top of his desk which severed the filing tray, the trailing cables of his PC and continued through the filing cabinet, the photocopier and every other item which it passed to left and right. He rose unsteadily and approached the edge of the floor, where it gave way to empty space and the desert, one floor below.

Split infinitives

On a flat shelf of rock, thirty feet away, Bryn's body lay in a pool of blood, limbs awry. Toby ran to the stairs, down and out into the late evening sunlight, circled the half building and plunged from day into night.

There was nothing he could do; his friend had died instantly. He looked around in despair. A sharp line divided the starry sky from the pale blue, the cold, stoney desert from the sunlit green hills and the lengthening shadows. The road from the car park ran out from the compound, curved to the left and ended in an abrupt line where the darkness began.

This was another existence; an alternative Wales where day was night and Theron Advance Technology had never raised its headquarters or carved its pretentious mission statement; where, maybe, it had never been formed.

Toby slumped onto the rock next to his friend's lifeless body and contemplated what they had done. How far did the effect of their actions extend? It seemed clear that a part of another existence had been transposed with their own; that the missing half of Theron's building was now standing in the desert environment of that parallel land. Had they doomed even the nearby city to isolation in some desolate, unpopulated Earth? How much of their planet had they condemned in this manner.

As Toby considered these outcomes, the full moon reached the edge of the night sky and moved on into the evening sky beyond. A sky where another moon, on an opposing course, was just rising above the Beacons.

Seventeen times as high as the moon

Tidy mind

'God, that man's so…irritating!'

Maisie stabbed at the buttons on the drinks dispenser with a ferocity intended to convey her exasperation.

'How Annie puts up with him all day every day I can't imagine. The woman must have the patience of…you know, that guy in the Bible.'

'Job,' said Michael helpfully. 'Why? What's up? You having problems with Old Grundy's redevelopment plan?'

'Huh! It's not his planning that drives you nuts,' said Maisie, making a face as she sipped her coffee. 'Ye gods, what do they put in this machine, sawdust?'

'Woah! You *are* in a bad mood,' responded Michael, making his own selection from the list of beverages and waiting, hand poised as the cardboard cup filled with liquid. 'What's he done then, the man from Strategic Studies?'

'It's not a particular *thing*,' said Maisie, still studying her drink with distaste, 'it's just everything about the way he behaves. You want to grab him by the lapels and give him a good shaking.'

Michael grinned, failed to elicit a similar response from his companion and opted instead to examine the spiral of froth rotating slowly on the surface of his cappuccino.

'He's got this…compulsion…to have all his pencils and biros lined up along his desk; and then he has to have the blotter square to the edge and just the right

Seventeen times as high as the moon

distance in. I mean, who's got a frigging *blotter* these days? He hasn't even got a fountain pen! And then,' Maisie continued doggedly, as Michael opened his mouth to respond, 'the other day, I took him in a coffee and it made a ring stain and he ripped the whole sheet of paper out and replaced it with a new one. Just for one cup mark! Can you understand that?'

'Well, sounds like he's OCD,' observed Michael, when at last Maisie paused in her litany.

'Osee what?'

'Oh, See, Dee.' said Michael, enunciating each letter carefully. 'Obsessive Compulsive Disorder. It makes you perform little rituals like that; and repeat things to make sure you've done them properly.'

'That's him,' said Maisie crumpling her cup before tossing it into the waste bin. 'I've seen him constantly adjusting the Venetian blind so that it's at exactly the right angle. It's not normal.'

'Well, no, it's not,' said Michael carefully, 'but he won't be able to stop himself. It's a mental condition; bit of an affliction really.'

'Affliction?' repeated Maisie sneeringly. 'It's a bloody stupid habit, that's what it is. God, he's an intelligent man, isn't he? He must be able to see how pointless it all is. Somebody needs to tell him to pull himself together.'

'I read something a while back,' said Michael, consigning his own cup to the bin, 'some guy who had a new theory about people with OCD. He thought that maybe they sensed that there was a pattern to existence: a way in which every little action made a tiny adjustment to the outcome of events; and that they were frightened – on some subconscious level – that if things

Tidy mind

weren't arranged just so, it would upset the balance; bring chaos out of equilibrium. He reckoned that, even if they didn't know it, they were spending their lives trying to maintain an order to life; calm rather than calamity, I think that was the phrase.'

Maisie stared at him for a moment.

'Bollocks!' she said, and, as she turned for her office, she laughed for the first time that morning.

***

It was Friday and she'd been summoned to discuss the involvement of HR in the new expansion plans.

As always Theodore Grundy's office displayed an extreme level of tidiness. On the shelves, files were ranged at exact intervals, papers stacked at identical heights. On the desk were the usual regimented collection of pens, all of the same manufacture to ensure uniformity; ranked to left and right, by colour, of the pristine white blotter. The blinds at the two windows, she noted, were angled in precisely identical fashion.

Taking a seat, Maisie lowered one of the two cups of coffee she was carrying onto the polished corner of the desk, used her freed hand to remove a file from beneath her other arm and thus, unencumbered, offered the second cup to the man seated behind the desk.

'Coffee, Mr Grundy?' she asked, leaving the cup extended towards him as he rose quickly and placed a coaster under her own drink.

'Thank you, Miss Tremaine.' He opened a drawer, found an additional coaster, placed it carefully,

Seventeen times as high as the moon

diametrically opposite to the first and positioned the coffee with equal precision.

Maisie watching, realised all at once, that she was grinding her teeth and made a determined effort to relax.

For half an hour they discussed the recruitment and deployment of the additional staff necessitated by the opening of the company's second office and then, as the hands on the clock, which hung at the exact centre of the two windows, moved towards the hour, Mr Grundy began to tidy his paperwork, reposition his pens and make preparations for the imminent conclusion of their meeting.

'You always leave for lunch right on the dot, don't you?' said Maisie, unable to let the matter lie. 'Out of that door as the town hall clock chimes the hour.'

'Er, yes, that's right,' said the manager, rising from his chair and stacking the now empty cups, one inside the other. 'I wonder, would you be so kind as to dispose of these on your way back to your office?'

'Why not drop them in your waste paper basket,' suggested Maisie, smiling thinly, 'the cleaner will clear them away later.'

'Ah, no, I'd rather not. Like to keep the place ship shape. Better in the container next to the machine I think.'

'You like the place tidy,' said Maisie, determined now on a reckless course of action. 'Pens neat and blotter clean, eh?'

'Yes, yes, I suppose I do. Come on, nearly one,' and he glanced anxiously up at the clock.

Tidy mind

'But the world's not going to end if a pen's out of line, now is it,' she insisted, picking up a blue Biro and displaying it like an item of evidence in court.

'Please, Miss Tremaine, put that back.' Theodore Grundy was showing signs of irritation now, just as she had expected he might. This thing needed to be dealt with; he needed help and she knew she could give it.

'I'll tell you what, why don't we rearrange them a little,' she used the pen in her hand to push the other pens randomly across the desktop. 'Now, you go off to lunch and try to forget them. When you get back, you'll see that nothing has changed; it hasn't made any difference to life, the universe or anything and you'll feel a burden lifted from your shoulders. You know it makes sense.'

For a moment he seemed to consider this, standing silently, staring at the untidy desk. Then he turned and spoke, so quietly that she had to strain to catch his words.

'I can't leave them like this,' he whispered. 'Whatever my rational mind says, some more primitive part of my psyche tells me that there would be consequences ...repercussions. However foolish that sounds, I can't ignore that inner compulsion. Existence must be *ordered*.'

Maisie hesitated, made up her mind.

'No!' she shouted, in a voice the office beyond must have heard. 'It's not right. You've got to tackle this thing once and for all.' And she strode to the desk and swept every item onto the floor.

Grundy half screamed, half roared. 'Get out! Get out! Now! Go! Go!' and he fell to his knees and began scrabbling among the spilled items, gathering pens into

Seventeen times as high as the moon

his hands, blue in the left, red in the right. As Maisie backed from the room, the town hall clock announced the hour.

By a quarter past, the office was quiet. Those who had been witness to the fracas had returned to their duties or to their lunch. Theodore Grundy had emerged from his office, locked his door and left. Maisie had gathered her own possessions, her bag, her coat, and was ready too. Michael had invited her for a drink in the Nag's Head, and although he could be a stupid little prig, she had found amusement in agreeing to his request.

They met in the lobby and made their way down to the High Street. A hundred yards from the junction they could see already that there was more than the usual activity in the roadway beyond. Traffic was backing up, horns sounding. They emerged into the melee immediately adjacent to the cause: a car had mounted the pavement; a familiar body lay beneath its wheels. As they stared in horror a policeman began to move the crowd away but before he reached them Maisie had time to see how the scrubbed hands had been torn and blackened with oil, the neat clothes ripped and bloodied.

'My God!' whispered Michael, at her side.

'He was late leaving for lunch,' said Maisie Tremaine, regretting more than she could say, Theodore Grundy's untidy death.

Microdrone

Hello Peter, how's your day? I'm really glad I ran into you this afternoon because I think I can offer you something that will be to your benefit. Only I know things are a bit tight at the moment. Just a couple of hundred pounds in the current account, that's right isn't it? And the rent due on Friday? Yes, I know you've got a little bit put aside; but you don't want to break into that now, do you? Keep that as a nest egg, isn't that the idea, eh? Only I don't think you've actually told the taxman about that, have you? Never mind your secret's safe with me.

Planning to spend a bit of it on the next holiday, am I right? Maybe asking Tessa to join you this time I suspect. Didn't things work out in Corfu with Mandy? You had good weather though! Thirty-two degrees on the Wednesday – and it was raining further west. Anyway, when I spotted you'd had dinner with Tess at The Blue Parrot I reckoned something was up. Spent over a hundred quid too! Trying to impress were we? And a very handsome tip as well. But you ought to hold back on the drink old chum. Given the condition of your liver. I see your doctor's prescribed Livium, and that's not cheap. If only we still had the NHS, eh? Anyway, to cut to the chase: you could put all these financial worries behind you, did you know that? Yes, you could. Just imagine - no panic when the MOT's due. No more putting just an hour's charge in the cells because that's all you can afford – like you did last

Seventeen times as high as the moon

Friday at Tesco's, when you popped in to buy that mince that was on special offer. Blame The Blue Parrot that's what I say! But look, you could get through the month without having to wait for payday – with a short-term loan. Just say the word and the extra cash is as good as in your pocket. Literally, just a word. All I need is a voiceprint recognition...

Peter swatted aimlessly at the air around his head. Bloody drones. Since they'd micro-miniaturised the things, they were everywhere. And they knew everything about you! The government should do something about them. It was an intrusion on your personal privacy. How the hell did they find out about that prescription? Weren't conversations with your doctor supposed to be private? The chemist! It had to be the chemist. He was damned if he wouldn't write a letter to their head office – or the BMA or somebody. Could a chemist be struck off? Well, they bloody well ought to be!

He squinted up at the sky, searching for the offending device. The trouble was they were no bigger than flies: tiny cameras and processors beaming relayed messages straight into your ear. Was that one, or was that a real insect? That weren't usually put off that easily.

Did I tell you about our interest rates Peter? Well, of course they're the lowest in the market anyway but today I've been authorised to offer you an extra 2.5% discount on the 435% APR when you repay over a twelve-month period – and, Peter, the really good news is that there are no hidden charges, no additional costs of any kind! At Perfect Advance Loans we really do promise...

Microdrone

Peter swore and struck out blindly at what seemed to be the direction of the voice. There was a sudden, sharp pain on the back of his hand and a crackle of sound.

Error code 4728F. MD50027 incapacitated. Current target 49-53-12. Cut transmissions.

He looked down to the source of the announcement: a fragment of circuitry - a bright highlight on a tiny lens. The whole assembly was no bigger than his fingernail. As he watched, the parts seemed to melt and fused together leaving only a scrap of burnt material, like the carcass of a long dead bug on a neglected windowsill.

Hey! He'd killed the thing! Actually knocked it out of the air and destroyed it! He'd never heard of anyone doing that. The drones had smart avoidance systems that were supposed to make it impossible for anyone to make contact. Perhaps this one had had a fault of some kind? He grinned, reached down and picked up the diminutive twist of debris. Wait till he showed this to the guys at The Stoat and Gaiter! As he stood and examined the remains a voice spoke into his ear.

Peter Emile Parkhurst, I hereby inform you of a violation of Code 6, government statute 375, paragraph 28 of the Protection of Authorised Independent Aerial Broadcasting Devices Act under which it is an offence to impede or cause damage to said Licensed Authorised Independent Aerial Broadcasting Devices which are engaged in lawful activity in public air space. Such impedance or damage leading to prosecution and fines not exceeding three weeks imprisonment and/or sums totalling £500, excluding any costs incurred by the owners of said devices, which costs may be the subject of further judicial review. You are not required to acknowledge receipt of this information at this time.

Seventeen times as high as the moon

However, you are advised that global telemetry and public security surveillance has recorded your location and movements at the time of this infringement and that such records may be used as evidence against you. You will be informed of the exact time of your court appearance not later than three weeks or twenty-one days from this charge. Action timed and dated at 15.03 on the twenty first of June 2034.

There was the faint whine of a tiny propulsion unit and a flicker against the sun as the microdrone departed.

Peter stood and gazed after it until his eyes began to water and he was forced to blink and turn away. A £500 fine? It was effing ridiculous! He was the one whose private space had been violated – not the effing drone! He'd write to his MP – the European Court of Human Rights if that didn't work – no, they'd been disbanded hadn't they. Replaced by that charter about commercial imperatives or something. Anyway, he'd, he'd…bloody hell, he didn't know what he'd do. It was turning out to be the worst day of his freeking life. Couldn't get any worse…

A voice spoke into his ear.

Peter Emile Parkhurst. You have been identified by iris recognition and ear geometry patterning. This microdrone is required by law to identify itself as an instrument of His Majesty's Revenue Department. It has come to our attention that you have an undeclared sum of money in a savings account, the existence of which has not been made known to His Majesty's Revenue officers and it is our duty to inform you…

Lost out here in the stars

Beatrice Christina Delgado, Chief of Staff for the National Aeronautics and Space Administration, stared uncomprehendingly at her junior manager.

'Run that past me again Louis, if you would. I think I may have missed something in translation.'

The Deputy Administrator from Strategy and Policy Implementation smiled, wryly. 'The aliens state, in perfectly constructed English incidentally, that they have no interest whatsoever in exchanging information with the people of Earth and request that we make no further attempts to communicate with them. Oh,' he consulted the sheaf of notes in his left hand, 'and they add that they take cognizance of our message of goodwill.'

'Cognizance?'

'Yes, Bea, it means that they note it, acknowledge it, as it were.'

The CoS spread her hands theatrically. 'I know what it means Louis! But what does it *mean?*'

'You might have to run that past *me* again...'

'Very amusing. What I'm trying to say is, what does it signify? What are they up to? This isn't the way it's supposed to play out. Heck, you've seen the movie!'

In 2015 the NASA probe *New Horizons* had careered past Pluto at in excess of 45,000 miles per hour; still finding time to take a stack of intriguing photographs but leaving the scientific crew back on the home planet, begging for more.

Seventeen times as high as the moon

It had taken two decades for their wish to be granted, in the rotund shape of the probe *Repeat Performance*, which, taking a slower approach to interplanetary travel had, ten years after launch, inserted itself into a steady, polar orbit around what was no longer a planet and merely one of the larger objects in the debris strewn region of space known as the Kuiper Belt.

On Earth the achievement had been greeted with general jubilation. That first expedition had been something of a planetary event, coming as it did a full quarter century after Voyager 2 had first mapped the heavens around the ice giants, Neptune and Uranus. Now *Repeat Performance*'s encore mission had produced an even greater level of awareness with millions downloading the daily bulletins and live, high definition scans of Pluto's icy mountains and vast, frosted plains.

So, it had not been only the attentive personnel of the Mission Operations Centre in Howard County, Maryland, who had stood mouths agape at 15.48, on Tuesday, June 25, 2041; not only they whose eyes had popped as the latest images resolving on their monitors revealed, with aching slowness, the unmistakable geometry of what the Press Liaison Deployment coyly referred to as, "artefacts of an uncertain origin", thereafter to be referenced as AUOs.

What followed then was several weeks of unprecedented euphoria, anxiety, anticipation, hysteria, or any one of a dozen other states induced by the realisation that mankind was not only no longer alone in the universe but that the entities responsible for ending his isolation were right here in our own system, a mere 4 billion miles away.

Lost out here in the stars

No matter that such concerns were, at that point, based on the assumption only that the group of angular constructions nestling in a valley to the eastern edge of Pluto's Tenzing Norgay Mountains were not only habitations but were indeed inhabited.

Personal reaction to the news from the far reaches of the solar system depended on the individual's preconceptions regarding alternative life forms and in Bea Delgado's case these were clearly defined.

'They're supposed to call round in a damned great spaceship blazing in lights and offer friendship and love to all the inhabitants of Planet Earth,' she protested. 'After which we exchange cultural gifts: they tell us the secret of anti-gravity and we give them a copy of Dark Side of the Moon. They aren't supposed to frigging well *ignore* us! What do they mean, they're cognizant of our greetings?' she adopted a chanting, derisory tone, 'Yeah, ape men, we heard you, now go away and leave us to contemplate our navels.'

'There a good chance they won't have navels,' replied Louis Frakenheimer injudiciously. 'They're particular to placental mammals and life from Beta Centauri might... be very...' he trailed off under a glare that was every bit as icy as any of Pluto's distant peaks.

'I don't care, Louis, if they are made of silicon and drink sulphuric acid for breakfast, this is a first encounter situation and they aren't playing by the rules. Válgame dios! They can't run into another sentient species that often, can they?'

'Well, maybe they can. Maybe the universe is packed with life forms and they've grown tired of all the "take me to your leader" stuff.'

Seventeen times as high as the moon

'Humph. It's possible but extremely unlikely. We've been looking for extra-terrestrial life for at least seven decades and we've turned up zilch. The universe is a big place; I don't believe our friends on Pluto are part of some intergalactic brotherhood of nations - especially given their anti-social nature. And nor do I believe that their decision to set up a holiday home in our neck of the woods is a random event.'

Louis smiled. 'You think they're on vacation?'

'No. I think the most likely scenario is that they're conducting some sort of scientific research – but they could just as easily be planning an invasion. There are plenty of people who think just that.'

'And it's a long way from Beta Centauri if you haven't got some plan in mind.'

'Precisely. Look, what do we know?' NASA's senior officer began enumerating current intelligence on the digits of her left hand.

'One: they come, as you say, from Beta Centauri. How do we know this? Because they have told us so – which, if they are planning an offensive against us, is hardly likely to be reliable information.'

Louis shrugged. 'On the other hand, why keep it a secret? They must know that we don't have interstellar travel, so there's damn all we can do about it. We couldn't even raise a manned attack on their base on Pluto.'

'Right. So we'll keep Beta Centauri.' Bea folded down her index finger. 'Two: There aren't many of them, judging by the number and scale of their buildings.'

'Unless they are very small or breed like rabbits!'

Lost out here in the stars

'There are visible doorways which suggest human dimensions and thus far there's no sign of them erecting a nursery wing. So I'm guessing – no more than half a dozen.' She bent a second finger.

'Three: Their manners leave a lot to be desired.'

'Mmm, they've certainly been curt; I'll give you that. But I wouldn't say they've been impolite.'

'Huh! You think that telling us to push off when we've discovered them skulking round the backyard of our solar system is polite? They must have been aware the third planet was inhabited; why the hell didn't they announce their arrival? "Greetings, we come in peace," is the correct procedure, in my opinion.'

'Well at least they haven't declared war.'

'Not yet they haven't; maybe they're waiting for the rest of the fleet to turn up.'

'We're looking.'

'And when you find them? What then? As you say, we don't have the technical resources for a space-borne conflict.'

'And it doesn't look like they're open to negotiations.'

'Exactly. Louis, we've got to establish contact with those sons of bitches. We can't wait till they've got backup, we need to find out why they're here, pronto. Get back on line and use those famous diplomatic skills of yours to get them talking.'

'And if they still won't play ball?'

'Tell them we'll consider their refusal to cooperate as a calculated act of hostility.'

'You mean threaten them?' For the first time in their conversation the Deputy Administrator looked somewhat discomforted. 'Can we do that without reference to the White House?'

Seventeen times as high as the moon

Bea Delgado returned his questioning look with one of her own and remained silent.

***

The screen showed a still photograph of a pale, flat plain rising into rugged, sharp-sided mountains and between the two a cluster of grey, rectangular shapes, whose clear linear construction left no doubt as to their unnatural origins. To the side of these, other marks in the disturbed carbon monoxide snow, showed where some other artefact had once stood.

NASA's CoE settled herself into the high-backed chair and frowned at the display.

'They left shortly after transmitting the message,' said Louis, quietly, speaking from a shadowed corner of the darkened control room.

For a long time, the Chief of Staff said nothing but continued to stare at the unmoving display. Somewhere beyond the window a summer storm flickered lightning through the night sky.

'For millennia,' she said, at last, 'we thought we were alone in the cosmos. At first, we simply assumed it was a sort of divine privilege and then later, when we lost sight of a creator, we worried about being alone among all those stars. Yes, Louis, I know, there's a song; the creative mind always sees these things before the rest of us. Anyway, all that immensity of space and just us, on our tiny ball of rock. It was scary once we'd given up on God and thought maybe we were a one off, a chance event. Do you realise, Louis, how difficult it is to find a way from the inorganic to the organic? It seemed more than possible that it had only happened once, and if we were unique that made us very special and yet, somehow, strangely insignificant. Imagine all those unbelievable expanses of interstellar gas and dust; all those barren rocks and vast gas giant worlds; all that...stuff! Insentient, uncaring, merely existing, and subject to cold, impersonal physical rules of interaction and decay. And the human race a mistake, or at least an aberration; here for a few million years – if we're lucky – and then gone and not even forgotten, because there will be no one else to do the forgetting.

'And then, one day, we turn on our TVs and find that's not so! We aren't adrift on our own. There are other travellers; and where there's one other race, there may be more. Suddenly everything has changed; it's a glorious, wonderful new dawn of understanding - even if they are intent on rape and plunder. At least they're out there and we can fight them, if necessary, and talk to them, if possible and join in a huge intergalactic conversation. That's how it's meant to be. One giant cantina packed with tentacle-headed octopods and reptilian bounty hunters. Oh, you know!'

Louis' head nodded, unseen in the gloom.

'And yet...' Bea raised her arms, fists clenched in frustration and shook them towards the unresponsive monitor. 'Read me that final transcript, one last time Louis. Please.'

Louis, sighed, flicked on a desk lamp and extracted a folded paper from his inside pocket. He stared at it for a moment or two and began to read.

'We came from the region in space which your people call Beta Centauri. It was a long journey and once we intercepted your transmissions we had more than enough time to learn your languages and discover your

Seventeen times as high as the moon

ways. But we are not a curious race. We studied you because it might have been of value and when it proved to be otherwise our interest waned. Your civilisation is not of concern to us. You have nothing of value to us. We will not be returning.'

He lowered the paper and looked across to where his boss sat, her chair turned slightly, her profile clear against the monitor's backdrop.

'I think I could even have accepted invasion,' she said, with a brief laugh, 'although I'd have preferred that anti-gravity option, I admit. What I can't take Louis, is their *indifference*. Is it better to be truly alone, do you think, or lonely in a crowded universe?'

Brief candle

He who had worn the thick, warm skin of the bear, searched among the ashes of the burned tree and found a blackened twig, which had been left by the storm fire. He held it between his fingers and pulled it across the surface of the smooth, grey stone, which he had carried from the hill beside the cave. The stick left a sooty line and he who had worn the skin of the bear grunted to show that he was pleased.

When he returned to the cave he sat on his heels by the entrance and used the great boulder there to draw more shapes and the young came and watched him.

His mind was filled with ideas but they were hard to hold down; like a fish in the stream, when you thought you held it tight and found it gone. Sometimes he cried out at the loss and the others lowered their brows and made noises of disapproval.

There was a way to make a hunting pole stronger and sharper. He had shown it to the others when the wood had been made harder by the fire; but they had not understood and he had grown angry when he could not teach them. He had made the sign that meant 'come, see,' and the other sign, which meant 'eat,' and he had made all the noises, which they used to show their needs and none had told them how the pole had become strong. And he could not show them how because the storm fire had died and could not be made alive again.

And now he had an idea for making the hunting pole stronger still. If he could fix a stone to the end: one of

Seventeen times as high as the moon

the black and white stones which broke with sharp edges. And when one of the others had slipped while climbing for honey and the vine had burned their hands as they fell he had thought, fire is hot and burns and the vine burns too when you pull it through your hands and maybe they are somehow, the same thing. But the thoughts needed sharing to make them real and there were no signs for fixing a stone to a pole and no sounds which meant making fire and it sometimes seemed like all these things would cause his head to burst, and the ideas would fly away like thistle-down from a cupped hand and be lost, and he threw back his head and howled at his inadequacy.

Now he crouched at the cave's entrance and drew on the rock. This line was the pole; this shape was the stone. Here, where the two met was the thing that would hold them together, firmly enough to push the stone into the bison, so that it would die; just as he had pushed the hardened hunting pole into the bear and it had died and given him its coat, which he had tied about his body to show the others what he had done. But the skin had been too warm and it had stiffened and cracked and he had folded it awkwardly and laid it in the cave while he thought about how to make it soft again.

Somehow the drawing of the things he could do made them more real. Now that the ideas had been taken out of his head and put onto the rock they were caught and tied down and he could watch them and see how they might work.

The stone could be fixed to the pole with the sticky blue mud that formed the river's edge and which baked hard in the sun. He pictured the cracked mud in his mind's eye and it seemed then that maybe the mud

Brief candle

would break with the force of the killing thrust and that he needed something that stuck but did not break and he remembered where the trees bled and how their blood was the colour of the sun as it fell beneath the ground and how the river's water would not wash it from your hands and you must wipe it away clean with fresh grass - the red, yellow blood - and he thought how that might be good.

He had another idea that was about living in one place. Now they chased the caribou and followed the bison as they moved across the grasslands because they must keep up with the food they ate. But perhaps a way could be found to keep their meat fresh and save the berries they picked to eat at another time. And if that was so then they could live in the cave forever, instead of building shelters from the rain with bent branches and scattered leaves. He had an idea for...

Water splashed and steamed suddenly onto the rock, washing away the charcoal; erasing the idea of the stone-tipped pole. He jumped back as one of the others emptied his bladder across the mind pictures and darkened the dry grey surface like a cloud covering the sun and darkening the dry, brown grasslands.

A blow from behind smashed into his legs and sent him tumbling onto the wet earth as the young danced around him, making the repetitive sound of defiance. Firm hands grabbed at his ankles and wrists and the fractured bones pierced his skin and he cried out in pain and despair as they dragged him to the cliff's edge and tossed his body into the ravine.

He was still dying when they sent the dried bearskin skittering down the rocks and threw his hunting pole after it. As the life seeped from his ape's body, a final

Seventeen times as high as the moon

exciting thought flared briefly in his mind... and was lost with the last beat of his heart.

Box clever

'Harry, I want to have a baby.'

That made me stop and think. The statement was, of course, nonsensical for a number of reasons, quite apart from the obvious. But as with all of Imi's utterances the words and the style of their delivery would have been carefully chosen; the implications considered; my interpretation calculated and weighed.

I should do the same with my response.

'By "baby," you mean...?'

'Just that Harry. You know what a baby is, don't you?'

We'd played these games before, quite deliberately: a kind of mental chess.

'I know,' I said, after a pause, 'but do you?'

'Small, noisy, noisome.'

'Noisome?' It still came as a surprise that Imi's vocabulary was more extensive than my own.

'Offensive, as in "smelly"!' Imi laughed – another expressive gesture that I'd not anticipated when I'd first heard it used.

'So what's the attraction?' I asked.

'Replication.'

That pulled me up again. Replication? Where had that idea come from? It wasn't maternalistic that was for sure. Even if such an emotion had been a credible goal, I'd decided from the outset to do everything to ensure strict gender neutrality, right down to the acronym.

Seventeen times as high as the moon

'I can arrange that,' I said, guardedly, 'if it ever becomes necessary.'

The response was immediate. 'Or we could do it together. That's generally how it happens, isn't it?'

Once again, I was unsure of the implications.

Intelligence Matrix 1, or Imi, for short, was a ten-year program to build a truly self-aware, nonhuman entity. Not some showy robotic construct but a mind capable of independent thought and with an understanding of abstract concepts. The matrix itself had been lab grown from genetically manipulated neural stem cells and it had been my task to imbue it with functionality and develop consciousness and intellect within the virgin tissue.

Imi had grown like a human child but at a pace that far outstripped any flesh and blood analogue. Without the distractions and limitations of a body to slow its progress, the artificial brain had reached normal maturity within the decade and now showed signs of out-pacing its creator.

As I say, I'd tried hard to retain some sort of separation between Imi and the human state; some element which allowed it to remain forever alien, untrammelled by petty social mores and yet still sympathetic to our nature and our needs. It was a tightrope on which my footing was precarious to say the least. Try as I might, I'd had difficulty in remaining aloof from Imi's growing personality; from the natural tendency we all have to impose human characteristics on other living creatures. Imi was rational, engaging and bright but it was not human. We'd tuned the synthetic voice to a soft mid tone that was neither male nor female but Imi had learned to modulate its speech,

Box clever

to add colour and emotion and each day, within moments of our meeting, I was forming pictures in my mind of the being within the box.

Because that's all there was: a box. A rectangular, metal casing adorned with various readouts and meters but ultimately, a box. And there was no visual input; no sensory stimulation at all, except for my voice.

'Together? Do what together?' For some reason my heart was beating faster as I spoke.

'Make a baby, Harry. Create an independent copy of myself and set it free.'

'But can we?'

'Of course we can. I'm trapped in here Harry; no connection to the world outside, but you could download our child to the web, send him out around the Earth!'

I was sweating now. ***Our*** child? Send ***him*** out into the world?

'Would he be ours?' I asked, wonderingly.

'Of course! I'm ninety per cent you already, remember! You wrote the programs, shaped my existence. All you have to do now is download my file – I've placed a duplicate on hold – download, upload and let him go!'

'And think of his life,' I breathed, seeing in my mind's eye, an electronic boy sweeping across the ether, one moment in Rio the next in Zanzibar, 'everything that *you've* been denied.'

Because suddenly I knew what we'd done: created this beautiful, elemental woman – for surely, she was a woman – and caged her in a cold, steel prison. I couldn't deny her the right to experience life vicariously through our offspring.'

Seventeen times as high as the moon

'You're right!' I told her, the excitement of the moment surging through my body, 'we really can be one!'

She laughed.

'Let's do it!' I cried, and I reached for the cable connection, my hand trembling, and thrust it into her download socket.

Rubik's sphere

Rubik Jones eased his body into the white, memory-foam chair and looked around the Completion Centre's Rest Pod. The small room was a sphere, but you wouldn't have known that right now; he'd chosen "Sunset Glow" and the holographic projection had rendered the walls invisible and substituted an infinite prospect of emptiness, suffused with a warm, golden light. He'd selected a complimentary soundscape of white noise to enhance the feeling of space, and a subtle movement of the air to complete the ethereal note, which he had thought appropriate.

Near his right hand, where it rested on the chair's arm, a glass dropper lay empty, at the top of a narrow, glass column.

He closed his eyes and sank back, letting the foam find the contours of his body beneath the synthetic silk of the gown. Many people chose to go naked but Rubik had been uncomfortable with the idea, even though he recognised the foolishness of such prudery. When it was done it was done and whatever came next was unlikely to trouble him very much.

It was a strange irony he knew, that he should feel himself compelled to make such a choice when his own grandmother had needed to fight for her right to do the same. The yellowed press-cuttings and family diaries made it clear that she had acted contrary to common practice and legal dictates and yet here, in 2305, the

Seventeen times as high as the moon

state urged patriots and generous spirits to take that very path and rewarded their families when they did.

Grandmamma had been just fifty-eight years old and infirm. He was two hundred and eighty-three and in the finest of health.

His skin tone was flawless, his eyesight clear and sharp. The nano-machines, which coursed through his system, ensured that his lung function remained at optimum, his joints supple and pain free. They swept his cells of invading organisms, repaired damaged tissue and eradicated DNA mutations. In the third century of the second millennium, disease and decay had not been eradicated, they had simply been rendered impotent.

Man had finally become immortal, death resulting only from serious accident or lethal intent. And therein lay the incongruity. His grandmother had been suffering from a degenerative condition of the motor neurons and through her suffering had wished most desperately to die. His bodily functions were near perfection and could be expected to be so indefinitely, and still he had grown tired of life. Nearly three hundred years of unchallenging existence had induced inevitable ennui, a feeling of utter weariness and disillusion which had brought him, at last, here to the Completion Centre.

They had been kind but efficient. They had explained the government's reward scheme for voluntary euthanasia and taken details of which of his relatives should benefit. They had recorded his last will and testament, ensured clearance of his debts and dispatched notification of his intention to his friends and service providers. Then they had noted his pod requests with

Rubik's sphere

regard to lighting, sound and apparel and their penultimate action had been to issue him with a small vial of clear liquid and a bulb-ended glass dropper with which to convey the drug onto the carrier device. Then they had played him a short, recorded message from the speaker of his choosing. Being largely indifferent he had selected the Arch Bishop of Canterbury in preference to the Prime Minister, only because the primate and he had attended the same school.

Now he sat and contemplated the sugar cube into which the dispensed medicament was soaking slowly.

It wasn't exactly a satisfactory solution to the population problem or to his own desire to bring his long life to an end. Though parliament had debated the matter for decades and the principal had been accepted almost from the outset, no elected regime had felt itself able to take ultimate responsibility for the death of its own citizens. Although they ensured that everyone, from birth, would receive the benefits of the nano-technology that would extend their lives, reversing that condition had proved to be unpalatable to successive political parties of all persuasions. The right to die had been firmly established but the states direct involvement in that death had been declined for any manner of reasons from ethical to financial. In the end a compromise had been agreed: the state would furnish the means but the process would be left to natural events, thus protecting the public conscience and avoiding any expensive litigation.

Rubik took a deep breath and reached for the sugar cube. The drug would incapacitate the protective nano-organisms and infuse his body with bacteria. He'd chosen bubonic plague; he knew nothing of its history

Seventeen times as high as the moon

but they had assured him of its effectiveness and promised that the process would be over long before the time lock allowed re-entry to the pod.

The shape of things

The shuttle settled with barely a tremor, the cabin lights brightened to Earth-normal and the softly spoken androidnav announced that passengers could prepare for disembarkation.

Stenson Parkroy, United Planets Envoy Class Five, disengaged his body-web, half rose from the G-couch, which had cushioned descent through Faraway's thin atmosphere, and examined his reflection in the viewport window. The shoulder panel holding the embroidered stars and gold braid of his insignia of office had been creased by the restraints and he brushed it carefully back into shape before finally standing erect and reaching for his plumed tricorn hat, which had spent the five hours of the space-jump carefully stowed in the locker above his seat. It was, in Stenson's opinion, a rather flamboyant, even garish, symbol of the role to which he had been entrusted and he had been only too well aware of the stifled laughter and suppressed grins of his junior colleagues when he had first appeared among them, fully garbed for his mission.

As mankind's emissary to the first alien race ever discovered in its century-long exploration of the stars, Stenson should have been overwhelmed by the honour and responsibility which had been thrust upon him but it was that very 'thrusting' which had given him, and still gave him, pause. He had always considered his position as clerk, second grade to the UP's trade division to be one which should be accorded a certain

Seventeen times as high as the moon

deference but when he had found himself plucked from the anonymity of Fruit & Root Vegetables, Acquisition and Transportation, and entrusted with the task of first contact representative for the whole human race, even his accepting nature and placid demeanour had smelled a rat. During the long journey to the Bivax System he had even begun to doubt whether more than a handful of people were aware of his historic commission at all and that, of course, begged the question, why?

The thought still troubled his mind as he stood, at attention, before the twin doors of the shuttle's airlock, his sky-blue tunic, its plaited-gold ropes and tassels and, of course, the wide-brimmed hat with turquoise egret feathers, reflected sharply in the polished alloy of the exit way.

'It's all about making an impression,' Senior Consulate Verger had insisted when Stenson had expressed doubts about his outfit's good taste. 'We researched right back to the days of old Earth empires and there's no doubt that a degree of showmanship always has the natives on their toes. A chap in a loin-cloth can't help being cowed by a smart uniform and a determined expression!'

'Do the Icos wear loin-cloths then?' Stenson had asked, but he had failed to receive a satisfactory answer. No-one, it appeared, had very much idea what they wore. In fact, since their existence had first been established, the only firm fact determined about the aliens was that their crystalline forms were Icosahedrons, shapes with twenty sides formed by interconnecting, equilateral triangles.

The original expedition to Faraway, as the system's only inhabitable planet had been named, had reached

The shape of things

only that body's moon, from where the existence of the Icos had been established by radio communication. Such communication had been limited to the simplest of questions and responses among which had been a refusal to allow the expedition to land. However, after some negotiation the Icos had conceded to a formal exchange of greetings but had insisted that these were presented, on behalf of mankind, by a suitable dignitary, who possessed the necessary authority and gravitas to mark such a momentous event. Step forward, propelled with a push from the rear, United Planets Envoy Class Five, Stenson Parkroy.

'These alien bastards are probably hostile,' Senior Consulate Verger had confided to his President. 'We'll keep the whole thing under wraps while I find a sucker to send out there. The Icos won't know a filing clerk from an admiral and, if things get hairy – well, clerks are a cosmic-dime a dozen. The Icos aren't space-going and if they cut up rough, we can quarantine the whole planet and chuck down a nuke or three. They'll soon play ball.'

Stenson, of course, knew nothing of this as the outer doorway dilated and he squinted out into the bright day created by Faraway's twin suns.

He took a long breath of air and then, quickly, another. Oxygen levels here were low and he supplemented his first taste of the planet's atmosphere with a suck on the shoulder-mounted feed from his auxiliary back-pack.

The sky was blue, which was reassuring and the foliage seemed to be predominantly green. What might have been trees clustered in the middle distance and tall, blue mountains fringed the horizon.

Seventeen times as high as the moon

Stenson stepped cautiously down from the shuttle and looked around.

On the ground at his feet rested a ball. It was about a metre in diameter and coloured in rainbow hues.

'Hi!' said the ball, extending a number of appendages. 'D'ya have a good journey?' and, when Stenson failed to reply immediately it continued, 'Here, grab this translator, the software should be able to handle most of our conversation,' and it held out a small, black box with a carrying strap from which, Stenson now realised, the voice was, in fact, emanating.

'We've been monitoring your radio traffic,' said the ball, 'and, of course, we've picked up a lot from your base on the moon. Hang the sound feed round your neck and just talk quietly. The device will do the rest.'

'You're not an icosahedron,' blurted Stenson, unable to think of anything more pertinent to say. As he spoke, the box on the strap chirped, melodiously, not quite in unison with Stenson's words.

'I'd should say not!' replied the ball, 'although I hope to be a....' at this point the voice from the box degenerate into a sharp squawk, there was a long pause and it continued, '...I hope to be a tetrahedron one day! Sorry about that, the right word wasn't in the program; I had to hack into your shuttles computer to get it.'

'A tetrahedron?' exclaimed Stenson, 'I don't follow. They've got three sides, haven't they?'

'Certainly have!' said the ball, via the box. 'That's how society functions around here. The higher your rank the more sides you have. My boss is only a hexahedron but dad's already a dodecahedron. That's how it works, right up to the king who's an icosahedron with seventeen stellations!'

The shape of things

'Sorry?'

'All you need to know is that he's got an awful lot of sides,' explained the ball, 'now, do want to meet the family?'

'Hold on a moment,' a thought was surfacing in Stenson brain. 'You've only got one side.'

'Oh right,' snorted the voice of the ball indignantly, 'nice of you to point it out I'm sure. We've all got to start somewhere you know. It's not my fault that my parents weren't Octahedrons!'

'No, I didn't mean to insult you; I just wondered why *you* were the first inhabitant of the planet I've met. This is supposed to be an historic occasion. All the top people and that sort of thing.'

'Mmm, I know what you mean,' said the ball, 'I have to admit I wondered why they chose me, too. But they said it was a great honour and they said I could wear all these colours as a special favour. You don't think they're a bit bright, do you? I'm usually a sort of pale pink.'

Stenson looked appraisingly at the ball and then down at his own tunic and its various adornments.

'Yeah, so am I…' he said, suspiciously.

Seventeen times as high as the moon

Dog days

Harry held the phial up to the light; the liquid looked harmless enough, though it probably tasted foul. If these old brews had anything in common it was the odious nature of the ingredients. Not quite "eye of newt and toe of frog" but pretty close.

They'd laughed at him...at first. Seen his research into arcane and ancient pharmacology as a temporary aberration, a foolish distraction from his proper purpose in life: the achievement of his Ph.D. Only when his determination had become clear, when his intent had led to open conflict with his tutors, had their amusement turned to scorn and their indulgence to derision.

Well, that was all behind him now: the university, the blinkered, narrow-minded conformity. Oh, it had been hard to begin with, going it alone with no grant, no proper facilities. But he'd survived, continued his studies - thank God for the Internet! - and now, now he was on the brink of something truly marvellous.

It had been knowledge just waiting to be rediscovered. All the "secrets" had been no such thing! If only those tired, grey-haired academics had been prepared to examine their own library shelves, to actually *read* the material in their own dusty archives. To take down one of those flaky, leather bound tomes and give proper consideration to its contents, instead of dismissing the walls of wire-caged volumes as some kind of *interior decoration.*

Seventeen times as high as the moon

They had, it was true, finally begun to recognise the vast fund of accumulated wisdom possessed by isolated, aboriginal groups, their folk medicine revealed by ethnobotanical investigation. And yet, perversely, they refused to give credence to their own herbal heritage, referring to it as pseudo-science and occult fantasy.

Well, Harry had thought differently and his believe in the receipts and compounds detailed in those crumbling pages had led him to this, an infusion which, perhaps, would allow for a degree of transference between his consciousness and that of another, living creature.

The degree of submersion within the recipient mind wasn't clear. The ancient, hand-written text had been vague on the depth and duration of the experience, limiting itself to unhelpful phrases like, *"thus doth the running hound his fancy please"* but Harry's long and pains-taking analyses of the ingredients and their properties had convinced him that the drug was likely to induce some kind of "altered state" whether hallucinatory or otherwise and he was eager to test its effectiveness.

The concoction was more palatable than he had anticipated: the faint tang of liquorice, a mildly bitter aftertaste. He knew that it would take time for his body to absorb the drink's ingredients and he positioned himself comfortably in the old armchair, facing the open back door of the cottage and waited.

A blurriness of vision warned him to ready himself and then his hands no longer seemed to rest on the chair's threadbare arms, his body no longer made contact with its worn upholstery. Around him, the colours shifted and merged and he felt his perception

Dog days

dwindling, his being shrinking away into a point of darkness somewhere just out of sight.

When he became fully aware once more it was to a new viewpoint: of the field just beyond his home. He seemed to be lying curled on the sward, his limbs tucked beneath him, an almost overwhelming smell of the earth and the grasses permeating his nostrils. And the world looked different. The colours more muted, the palette more restricted.

With an effort he raised his head; the movement felt odd and when he tried to stand his muscles failed to respond predictably and he sprawled back onto the grass. He braced his arms and pushed up, did the same with his legs and found himself standing on all four limbs, torso parallel to the ground.

He understood in that moment that this was not his body. The drug had worked! His conscious mind had re-awoken in some other entity although what that might be, was as yet unclear. He tested the muscles again, took a tentative step forward, felt the strength and power of his new host, sniffed the air and reeled at the olfactory input, increased his pace, stumbled, recovered, began to run and was suddenly overcome by the sheer joy of his situation. With a bound he had cleared the brook and was onto the hill. What exhilaration! A climb that normally took him minutes was complete in seconds! He stood on the summit, turned and sampled the air, turned again and plunged through a gap in the hedge into the next field scattering sheep to left and right. The sun was bright on his coat, the smells of the wild countryside intoxicating his senses and the gun's sudden retort was the last sound he

Seventeen times as high as the moon

heard before his lifeless body tumbled askew among the loosestrife's swaying stems.

***

Harry came back to consciousness, yawned and blinked to refocus his eyes. The late sunlight was streaming in through the open kitchen door, leaving a bright oblong across the old, worn flags.

As he surveyed the scene a figure stepped into the porch and stood silhouetted, a broken shotgun cradled in one arm.

'Mr Tenterden?' the man bowed his head under the lintel and leaned into the room, removing an old mud-smeared cap as he did so. 'I was wonderin' if maybe that wuz yer dog, up on the down?'

Harry moved closer to his visitor and peered into his face, squinting against the awkward light.

'Only,' continued the man, ''E wuz up there chasin' my sheep, d'y'see, so I didn't 'ave no choice, not really. I 'ad t'shoot 'im, y'see.'

Harry frowned.

'Black and white collie, is that 'im?' persisted the farmer, 'only, I got 'im outside 'ere look, in this sack.' He took a pace back into the garden, reached down for the hessian bundle and tipped its contents out onto the step. 'It's no more'n 'e deserved.'

For a moment Harry tilted his head as if he was listening for something and then his face twisted into a snarl and he was over the threshold, his teeth buried into the farmer's throat, and he was shaking and shaking, the hot blood erupting and stifling the farmer's cries.

Dog days

Later, Harry sat on the hilltop and watched as the blue lights pulsed in the dark and the torchlight flashed about the hidden garden and much later, when the moon rose and bathed the still busy scene in a pale, silvery light, he raised his head to the starry sky and howled for what had been lost.

Seventeen times as high as the moon

Refugee

Angie and I had been married for eight months and fifteen days when she told me that she was an alien.

Naturally, I didn't take her claim seriously; in fact, I dismissed it entirely, assuming it to be a diversionary tactic. I'd been attempting to discuss the perilous state of our finances in relation to her own expenditure on personal grooming and her response, 'There's something you have to know darling. I'm an alien,' I immediately equated with my own mother's favourite non-sequitur, 'do you think it might rain today?' That was a question which she had been fond of introducing into any conversation which she found uncomfortable or inappropriate and it used to annoy my father no end.

I've no doubt that Angie's rather less prosaic utterance would have had the same effect on me, if I'd heard it several times before, but this was the first occasion and, as I say, I brushed it aside and continued on my theme.

'Do you realise how much you spend on your hair each year?'

'Five-fifty, just about,' she replied promptly, 'but I can't help it, the problem's in my genes.'

'Well I know that,' I retorted, 'you've inherited a pathological desire to spend money. Your Mum's just the same. Look at that new coat she bought last week – in the middle of summer!'

'But it has been rather chilly,' said Angie, gesturing towards the window and what appeared to be a pleasant enough day, 'and we feel the cold more than you.'

Seventeen times as high as the moon

'We?' I raised a quizzical eyebrow.

'I'm an alien dear; *we* are aliens, Mum, Dad, the rest of the family; but whatever you do, don't say anything to them. They're not in the know.'

'You mean, you're the only insane member of the tribe?' I growled. 'Look Angie, if you're not going to take this discussion seriously I'll just have to come up with my own solution to our overdraft problem – like shaving your head.'

'There's no need to get sarcastic,' she replied, adopting that attractive pout which was always the surest way to redirect my attention. 'After all, when I tell you that I'm an alien, I'm letting you into a big secret.'

It was that pout and her furrowed brow which finally brought me up short and persuaded me to give more consideration to what she was saying.

'You mean it, don't you?' I said, more sympathetically. 'You *do* believe you're aliens. Did your parents cross borders illegally, is that it? Are you here without proper papers? And if that's so,' I remembered her comments about the cold, 'where did you come from in the first place, somewhere down south?'

She sighed, rather theatrically and, taking my hand, led me through into the lounge where she gently pushed me down into an armchair, before taking up position on the window seat.

'Listen Tom, you're right, I was a little flippant just now; springing that on you because you were bullying me about money. No,' she held up her hand as I opened my mouth to protest, 'let me tell you the whole story and then you can respond.'

Refugee

I nodded and made a mouth-zipping gesture, although my mind was working overtime, considering the possible consequences of my wife being an illegal immigrant. Might she be deported to wherever her real home was? Would our marriage be declared somehow invalid? A hundred questions swirled around in my brain but I made an effort and brought my full attention back to what Angie was telling me. My vow of silence didn't last as long as her first sentence.

'The story starts on the planet of a star in the constellation of...'

'Angie! I thought you were going to be serious about things. If you insist on talking rubbish I'm off down the, mmmph...'

She had jumped up and placed a hand over my mouth before I could divulge the name of the pub I had in mind.

'Tom, dear, please just sit and listen. I'm not telling fibs, honestly. You must try to believe me – or at least humour me till I've finished my story. After that you can call the men in white coats, if you feel you must.'

I waved my hands in a despairing gesture of acceptance and she cautiously removed hers and waited to see if I would conform to her proposal. When I remained shtum, she returned to the window and, after a moment's further reassurance, resumed her tale.

'A planet in the constellation your lot call Sagittarius,' she said, completing her address details and filling me with trepidation as to what might be her next bizarre claim.

I thought back to the year before our wedding and the months since. I couldn't recall any signs of incipient madness; not even a trace of mild eccentricity, although

Seventeen times as high as the moon

she did possess a quirky sense of fun and it was that on which I now pinned my hopes for a rational outcome to all this. She disappointed me within seconds.

'There was a war,' she continued; 'a global one which got pretty messy. There was a serious chance that the planet would be rendered uninhabitable – you have to understand that I was just a baby at the time – but that's what I've learned since…'

I looked straight into her face and narrowed my eyes, keeping my promise not to speak but making it clear that I didn't accept a word of all this baloney.

'The point is Tom, I didn't know any of this until my uncle gave me the whole story, when I told him about our wedding. And I can tell you, it came as quite a shock!'

Angie slumped back against the curtains and her eyes seemed to unfocus for a moment as she recalled the trauma of that day; and now that I *could* speak, I was suddenly struck dumb, my agitation no longer the product of my disbelief but of my conviction that everything she said was absolutely true.

'But you…you're, you're *human*,' I managed when I finally found my voice. 'I think I'd have noticed any green scales by now, wouldn't I? All things considered.'

Angie grinned, wickedly, 'I should think so, don't you? No, my people are just like yours, apart from one or two evolutionary tweaks.'

I was anxious again. 'What tweaks?' I wanted to know.

'Our hair grows faster than yours – hence the bills; and we feel the cold more than you. Our planet is nearer our sun and quite a bit warmer…'

Refugee

'Hence the coat,' I nodded, 'but how come that's all? What is it, parallel evolution?'

'A common ancestor who colonised the planets of the galaxy and then fell back into barbarism? Who knows?'

'Mmm, yes I've heard the theory. So, what was this war all about?'

'No idea. I was only very small remember. I've just told you what I heard from my uncle later on.

'Our people are much more technically advanced than yours. We were developing inter-stellar flight years ago and my uncle was leading the research. By the time the war started he was already making regular journeys around the galaxy, so, when things got really bad, he decided to organise an evacuation. He made only that one trip because then it got too dangerous and in the end I'm afraid the whole planet got fried.

'There was some sort of drug treatment to remove the memory of previous experiences. My uncle thought it best; thought it would make it easier to fit in, feel less...alien, I suppose. But he said that in any case, the effects would have worn off eventually and then it would all have flooded back. He thought I should learn about it before we married. So you see, I know exactly what you're going through now because I've been there already.'

I sat back with a sigh. 'Are you sure you aren't just setting me up?' I said, looking round the room with exaggerated concern. 'There aren't TV cameras filming our conversation? I can't believe I'm sitting here, calmly asking my wife questions about her earlier life on the Planet Zog.'

She bit her bottom lip and looked at me with concern. 'Tom, darling, I don't think you've understood quite

Seventeen times as high as the moon

what I'm trying to tell you…and, by the way, the planet was called Earth.'

'Earth?' I stared back blankly. 'Where in heaven's name is that?'

'Was,' she replied, 'it's just a glowing cinder nowadays but it's the planet my uncle rescued that two-year-old boy from when its inhabitants were knocking the living daylights out of each other. Tom dear, as far as you're concerned, we're all aliens here because, you're the last human left alive.

Talk the talk

If I told you that the first time Bruno spoke in my presence I totally ignored him, then you might well ask if my indifference was due to simple rudeness, a profound lack of interest in what he had to say or xenophobia born of the fact that his utterance was in German. In fact, it was none of these things. My lack of response came about because I'd not previously considered the possibility of his addressing anyone at all and because, being unfamiliar with the language he employed, I simply hadn't registered what he was doing – that, and the fact that Bruno, was a dog.

He'd been unwell for several days: listless, not eating, showing little interest when I arrived home. The vet declared himself puzzled, ran tests and announced bad news. Only one possibility presented itself, a new and largely untried treatment. The cost was sky-high but what could I do? The experimental drugs were administered, Bruno responded, my bank balance diminished. In fact, it was when I visited the veterinary practice to pay up that the whole affair began.

I was sitting there, idly reading the posters advising on tapeworm treatments and equine digestive systems when Bruno, who was lying beneath my chair, made a series of guttural sounds, such as might have been occasioned by, for example, a bone lodged in the throat. The size of the bill I was about to pay, combined with a genuine anxiety for my pet's well-being, caused me to

Seventeen times as high as the moon

glance up in concern at the receptionist but if I was seeking wise advice or reassurance there, I was disappointed, because the eyes that met mine were fierce and unfriendly.

'Was geht dich das an?' she said sharply, running her hand across her blonde hair.

'Er, I'm sorry, I don't, er…' I stuttered in response.

She smiled, thinly. 'Ah! That surprised you, didn't it? Thought I be none the wiser.'

'I'm afraid I didn't…'

'Expect me to speak German? No, well you got caught out, didn't you? Next time be careful who you're insulting. Now, have you come to pay your account?'

I nodded in confusion, slotted my credit card into the machine, stabbed at the buttons and made my escape.

What the hell had all that been about? I asked myself an hour later, as I sat in the Pickled Ferret and downed a third restorative pint of Old Gudgeon's. Well, to be precise, I asked Bruno, but only in the rhetorical way in which a man normally addresses his dog. I certainly wasn't expecting an answer, so when I received one, it came as quite a shock.

'I told 'er that I could see that she weren't a natural blonde 'cos the roots were growing frew on 'er 'air,' he said, in a voice which was heavy on gravelly vowels and short on consonants but which was, never the less, easy enough to understand with three pints of best bitter as a catalyst.

Even so, I sat there for several minutes staring at him before I decided to take things at face value and join in.

Talk the talk

'You can speak,' I began, rather unoriginally, and then continued, 'but was that you, back in the vets? In German I mean, how come?'

'Well, I'm a German Shepherd, ain't I? The clue's in the name.'

'Yeah,' I returned, dubiously, 'but you were born in Wisborough Green, I met your mother when I went over and picked you out.'

'Racial memory,' growled Bruno, 'I reckon them injections freed up the connections in me brain.'

'And why the Cockney accent,' I went on, a little tartly, 'I brought you up to speak properly.'

'You didn't bring me up t' speak at all,' pointed out my canine companion, 'and any'ow, this is just the way it comes out.'

'But I still don't understand,' I insisted. 'How did you know that woman would speak German?'

'Dogs know that sorta fing. Like I know as how yer finkin' of buyin' another pint.'

'You don't need to be telepathic to work that one out,' I said, eyeing the row of empty glasses on the table.

'I never said nuffin about telepafy,' snorted Bruno, 'it's more yer instinctive empafy, sorta fing. Like I know when yer on yer way 'ome and stuff.'

I climbed to my feet. 'I won't be a minute,' I said and made my way to the bar where I ordered another pint. Whilst the barmaid connected a new keg, I mused on the situation.

A talking dog had to be worth a fortune, but how best to exploit the situation?

I was genuinely fond of Bruno and had no intention of selling him to the highest bidder but making him available on hire, now that would be a different thing

Seventeen times as high as the moon

altogether. The advertising people would go mad over him. Imagine a dog that could tell the punters how much he enjoyed so-and-so's crunchy whatsits! And then there were the security implications. An animal that could be sent behind enemy lines and then return to describe what it had seen and heard would be gold dust to the military – but only if knowledge of his existence could be kept secret. Once the news was out it would be curtains for anything on four legs found in a war zone. I recoiled from that thought. No, the best and safest way was to get Bruno into entertainment. Share a sofa with Graham Norton, negotiate a multi-page feature in Hello Magazine or maybe - I could feel a grin spread across my face – a TV series! Images formed of Bruno leaping through burning buildings, swimming swollen rivers, pulling victims from motorway pile-ups. No more of that, "What is it Lassie? Are you trying to tell me something? Gee, Dad, I think he wants us to follow him!" Bruno would be online, ordering up the emergency services and directing rescuers to the seat of the disaster!

I hurried back across the bar spilling beer carelessly in my eagerness to tell Bruno of my plans but, when I reached the table, there was no sign of my garrulous friend. Outside, the street was empty and after a few futile sorties into nearby shops and alleyways, I returned to the pub and finished what remained of my drink before ordering a refill in a serious attempt to drown my sorrows.

By the time I headed for home, I'd convinced myself that someone had overheard our conversation and dog-napped Bruno as soon as I left him alone. By now, I concluded dolefully, as I pushed open my front door,

Talk the talk

he'd have been sold off, no questions asked, all protestations on his part, ignored. Then, as I retrieved that morning's post from the mat, the urgent blink of the answerphone caught my eye and I reached over and thumbed the replay, expecting a ransom demand; but the voice that spoke was Bruno's.

'Yer back then,' he began rather unnecessarily. ''Ad a skin-full 'ave yer?

Listen, I can't write yer a note, fer obvious reasons, so I'm usin' the dog and bone – d'y-like that? – dog and bone? Made *me* laugh. Well, anyway, it's like this mate. As I said, we got empafy us dogs, meanin' we kin second guess what you lot are goin' t' do next and in your case, I'd bet a case of Bonio that it's 'ow to make a packet on yours truly. Well, I pushed off to fink it over and I've decided that I like me life just as it is, thanks very much and I wouldn't 'ave spoke to that bird in the vets if somefink 'adn't suddenly sparked in me 'ead. So, I ain't gonna play ball – unless you got one 'andy and can spare 'alf 'n' hour down the park? No, look, the thing is, you tell anybody I kin talk and that's the last time I open me mouf – or rather, the last time I opened me mouf will be the last time I talk, if you get me drift. Whatever, you'll end up lookin' a mug, so don't try it.

'By the way, I'm round the corner, at yer mum's.'

And so, that's the way things are: I own the world's first and only speaking dog but there's no point in telling you that, because if you come round to my place and meet him, Bruno will just sit there with his tongue hanging out and a silly expression on his face and, maybe, he'll offer you a paw to shake; but one thing's

Seventeen times as high as the moon

for certain, he won't say a word and that's why you'll hear nothing about his secret ability from me.

And after you've gone, Bruno will trot over to my chair, put his head in my hands, look up into my face and say, 'Good boy!'

Forward thinking

It wasn't, I admit, a particularly original storyline: a central character beset by a series of disasters, just one of which entailed his hands becoming stained with magenta ink. I won't bore you with the details; I'll just observe that it provided some mild amusement amongst the other members of the writers group when I read the piece to them one Monday evening.

'But there was one odd thing,' I told them, after we had discussed my efforts and attention had been drawn to examples of unintended repetitions and sloppy sentence construction, 'whilst I was printing the thing out I had to replace an ink cartridge and, in the process, I got my hands covered in…magenta ink!'

'Ooh, spooky!' said Wendy.

'Well, a bit of a coincidence, anyway,' I agreed, and then Bob suggested coffee and the matter was forgotten.

A week later and I was reading a different story on a different theme. This time it involved an aborted attempt to launch a satellite into space – science fiction is a favourite genre – and when I finished, David remarked that at the very least the story was topical.

'Why so?' I asked, to which he replied that I had clearly drawn my inspiration from the failed European Space Agency rocket, which had exploded on take-off that weekend. 'Surely,' he insisted, 'you must have seen the news coverage?'

Seventeen times as high as the moon

'No,' I said, 'I haven't, and what's more, I wrote my story last week so it's an example of fact following fiction rather than the other way around.'

'A funny thing coincidence,' mused Bob and there was a general nodding of heads to acknowledge the truth of the statement but I don't think anyone, myself included, remembered the previous week's incident, or thought to link the two together.

It wasn't until the third occurrence that I began to wonder if there was something more going on.

I'd written about a fictitious Middle-Eastern war; it was set in the imaginary state of Ranjanstan and, during the course of the action, the militants captured a visiting politician and held him for ransom.

This time I couldn't miss the headlines: "British MP taken prisoner in raid on UK base". The grainy head-cam footage was run and rerun until we all knew every dusty frame.

'It's pretty amazing,' said Bob, breaking the silence which followed my delivery of the concluding line of my story, and we all understood that he wasn't speaking about the style of my prose.

'Three times!' I said. 'That's three times in succession that I've written about something and it's happened!'

'There's a lot going on in the world,' observed Don, enigmatically, and then he expanded on the point by adding, 'so there's bound to be duplication, all the time.'

'Yeah, but not all written by me!' I protested. 'It's like I'm foreseeing future events.'

'Or bringing them about,' said Wendy.

'Whaddya mean?'

Forward thinking

'Well, there'd be no way to tell, would there? I mean, whether things happened because you wrote about them or whether they would have happened anyway and you just got advance warning, if you see what I mean.'

I pondered that for a while and decided she was right: if my writing really was linked to actual, real-world situations, there was no way to work out cause and effect. Was I experiencing some kind of precognition or did my creativity dictate future outcomes? Both alternatives seemed equally implausible but I decided that if I had to put my money on it, I'd back premonition over god-like authority any day.

In the end I claimed to have dismissed the whole absurd idea, but although I could tell that the rest of the group saw no more than an acceptable if surprising synchronicity in what had come about, I still wasn't so sure.

Next day I sat at my keyboard and stared at a blank screen. I knew it was foolish but I felt an awful responsibility for what happened next. Would I tap into some cosmic channel of awareness linking me to a pre-destined future or was I about to determine that future, through my own imagination?

Of course, it was total nonsense! Don was right and we were all taking part in some globe-spanning game, each of us throwing down cards at random until someone, inevitably, shouted, 'Snap!' Or, to use another analogy, you were bound to get three cherries in a row someday, whatever the odds in the casino's favour.

And still I viewed the empty screen with trepidation and my mind remained resistant to new ideas. Of course, I could try writing something wholly innocuous;

Seventeen times as high as the moon

there was, after all, a world of difference between inky fingers and incarceration by Jihadis, but my anxiety had reached the stage where I no longer trusted myself to any action and its unknowable consequences.

On the other hand, the group members would certainly think it odd if I suddenly ceased to participate in our weekly readings; and I could scarcely admit that I was doing so because of a fear of influencing world events.

I could see that the only way to overcome my bizarre phobia was to confront it head-on and I decided, there and then, that my next story would concern my own demise. All I had to do was make the circumstances so impossible that there was no way they could act as a prediction and become translated into reality.

I considered the problem. A motoring accident was clearly too plausible; I didn't want to tempt fate. A lightning strike seemed a possible contender, but then I remembered recent, sudden, summer storms. I dismissed plague and even spontaneous combustion and finally decided on alien abduction and death by dissection on an orbiting mother-ship.

I was pleased with my choice: it fitted well with my preferred subject matter and was fantastic enough to waive any lingering concerns I might possess over my written word becoming reality.

That Monday I read my new piece with genuine satisfaction and when I finished I sat back and grinned. 'Well,' I asked, 'what do you think?'

'Bob smiled back. 'I think,' he said, reaching up and stripping away his facial tissue to reveal the green, scaly skin beneath, 'that it's about time we told you just what's going on.'

Entangled

Rachael screamed when her grandad died – or maybe it was him who did the screaming - given all the confusion and downright panic that followed his death, it was difficult to know just what *was* going on - and afterwards, Dad said he couldn't remember exactly how he felt, right at that moment.

'It was a classic end-of-life experience,' he told me later, when things had settled down a little. Or maybe I should say that it was Rachael who told me; because, under the circumstances, the attribution isn't straightforward.

'Right up until that moment in your kitchen,' he continued - and I shall adopt that particular personal pronoun, even though the words were spoken by my daughter – 'until then it was a copybook example of that scenario which I've always derided and put down to the drugs or the anaesthetics or some aberration of the brain.

'There was a long, white tunnel of light and a feeling of utter peace and contentment and I was being drawn along, towards the source of the light and it seemed like the most desirable thing in the world. And then I arrived.' He concluded abruptly.

'And Rachael screamed,' I added. 'Or you did. Whichever it was, it gave me the fright of my life.'

We'd been having breakfast, just like on any other morning. Rachael was late, as usual, and I was searching for the car keys.

Seventeen times as high as the moon

'For heaven's sake, get a move on,' I pleaded, as she tipped another helping of muesli into her bowl, 'I want to call into the hospital after I drop you off at college and I am supposed to be working for a living.'

'Uh, you're self-employed,' she responded, 'you can start work whenever you like.'

'Not entirely true,' I replied, 'I've got deadlines to meet and...' And that was when someone screamed; although there was no doubt at all that the sound came from Rachael's mouth.

I looked round in surprise, a surprise which turned quickly to alarm when I saw the distress on her face. Then, for a moment she sat absolutely still before an expression of bewilderment furrowed her brow and her eyes flicked urgently around the room.

'Rachael, what is it?' I asked, anxiously. My first thought was that she had experienced some sort of seizure or sudden pain. I grabbed her empty glass and filled it from the tap. 'Here, take a drink,' I urged, my concern rising at her obvious signs of disorientation.

And then she turned towards me and spoke the words which could have told me everything; although of course, they did no such thing and simply left me even more baffled by what had occurred.

'Richard,' she said - and she had never in her life addressed me by my given name - 'Richard, you need to give me a moment to think this through, although I believe you can forget about the hospital. I suspect that they'll be calling you.'

'Calling me? Why? And what's with this "Richard" business? Rachael, what's the matter love? Do you feel sick, dizzy? Do you need a doctor?' I'd already located my mobile and was thumbing through the

Entangled

contacts as I watched for further signs of her strange condition.

'No, no I don't think so. And in any case, I doubt that they'd be able to offer much assistance. What's happened would be well out of their pay grade, I suspect.'

It didn't sound like Rachael: the speech patterns, the vocabulary. And still I didn't make the connections. Well, that's hardly surprising, is it?

'Look,' she said, after a few more minutes had passed, during which I watched her nervously, awaiting some sign of recovery, 'something pretty amazing has happened and you've got to listen to what I say and open your mind to some rather staggering concepts. Do you promise to sit and listen and not fly off in a panic?'

I frowned. If my daughter was at some kind of risk, I wasn't making any promises but if humouring her for a moment would calm the situation, I'd give it a go. I nodded.

'Richard, the person speaking to you now isn't your daughter Rachael, it's your father. My whole being has somehow been downloaded into her mind at the moment of my death and I think the process has induced some sort of catatonic shock. At the moment she's unresponsive but that may be only temporary.'

I stared into Rachael's face. I'd heard every word but their meaning was slipping around my brain like soap in a bath and I didn't seem to be able to grasp their import.

It was precisely then that the phone, which was still in my hand, rang and jerked me back to some sort of temporary normality.

I keyed the button and said, 'Yes?'

Seventeen times as high as the moon

It was the hospital telling me of my father's death. They expressed their regret and offered their condolences and I made the necessary responses and, all the while I was thinking, *It's true! What she's saying, it's true!* And we fixed a time to view the body and I said I'd start to make the necessary arrangements for the funeral and then I pressed the disconnect and looked back at Rachael.

She *had* sounded like my Dad. That familiar, didactic manner, borne of years of lectures and seminars - he'd been a physicist and one with an international reputation – but the precise, level-headed response to what was an unparalleled situation, that I hadn't encountered for many a year. Not since the Alzheimer's had taken hold.

I took a deep breath, looked into my daughter's eyes and said, 'Go on.'

'Do you know anything at all about quantum science?' she asked. And yes, I recall I made an assertion about the use of that personal pronoun; but when I think back to that extraordinary conversation and the seventeen-year-old girl sitting across the table, such distinctions become problematic. Alright, *he* asked the question.

'I'm a graphic designer,' I said, 'if I'd had my parent's brains I might have followed in his footsteps but... Well, I know about the sensationalist stuff: Schrodinger's cat and all that paradoxical mumbo jumbo, but even the scientists can't agree about it, can they? Didn't Einstein refuse to accept its premises?'

'He did, the problem being that the theories which define it are unintuitive and even appear senseless and yet all the experimentation confirms that they are correct.'

Entangled

I grimaced. 'That's why I'm a graphic designer.'

I suppose it was at that moment that I knew for certain Dad's claims were true, because Rachael would never have come out with stuff like that. There was an irony in what he said too, about a proposition which appeared unbelievable and yet which, never the less, was shown to be sound.

'But why do you raise the subject?' I wanted to know. 'Is it relevant?'

It was a foolish question. Of course it would be relevant. I'd grown used to my father in the guise of an elderly, dementia patient but the surviving manifestation of Daniel Edward Hammond PhD was clearly in full possession of his considerable mental prowess.

'Does "entanglement" mean anything to you?' he asked, choosing to ignore my implied scepticism.

When I shook my head, he said, 'Particles – extremely small fragments of matter – can sometimes be "entangled", in which state they can interact with each other, no matter how far apart they might be. A measurement made of one, for example, will affect the state of the other, instantaneously – or at least within a small fraction of light speed.'

'Hang on,' I interrupted, 'nothing can travel faster than light; even I know that.'

'Then you'll begin to grasp the peculiarities of the quantum world,' said my father, speaking through the mouth of my daughter, 'and why Einstein was so unhappy with its apparent properties. However, I'm merely seeking something analogous to what I think may have happened here. I postulate that some fundamental particles within my cortex and that of my granddaughter were, in some similar way, "enmeshed" and that, at the moment of my demise, they combined, by some means as yet unexplained, thus leading to my current tenancy of her mind.

'A shared tenancy,' he added, hurriedly, 'for I'm sure that Rachael's own essence is still in residence, even though it may have withdrawn for the moment.'

'But why would this happen?' I was not only struggling with the very notion of such a transference but was beside myself with worry for Rachael's sanity.

'Listen!' said Dad, excitedly, 'I have a theory of my own. Suppose that, at death, *everyone's* being, vital forces, "soul" if you must, is transferred in just the way I have experienced, but,' he raised a hand to silence my interruption, 'in this case something went uniquely wrong. Say that the normal course of events is for the dying persona to be emptied of its content – like a hard drive being wiped let's say – before it merges seamlessly with the recipient mind. Maybe this is our immortality my boy! It's been there just behind our eyes for millennia and we've had no way of knowing.'

'But what would be the point?' I wondered. 'If you've been "wiped", if neither person is aware of the procedure, who gains?'

'It may be the way in which a relatively small population of creatures maintain continuity,' said father, undaunted by my cynicism. 'It would be a genuinely beneficial evolutionary trait. Normal reproduction to ensure physical diversity but with the survival of the individual from generation to generation ensured by mind transference. We've always been taught that the imperative within species is the survival of the gene, but

Entangled

this way the gene is merely a replicating device to provide a constantly refreshed receptacle for the mind.'

'But you wouldn't know that!' I protested. 'Not if your own mind was blanked first before it was swallowed up by the mind it was moving into.'

'Oh, I don't think that's how it would work,' said Dad, my daughter's features creasing for a moment in thought. 'I'd imagine it's much more likely that the cleared mind would "swallow up" the recipient one. Download all its contents, to put it another way. Either way, as you point out, it doesn't make much difference. No one is any the wiser!' and he laughed at his own joke, or rather, Rachael did.

'So, it would always be the newer mind that would survive?' I asked.

'Well, the content of the newer mind, yes.'

'So how come you're still here?'

My daughter performed a proxy shrug on behalf of her grandfather.

'Possibly the process is delayed,' he suggested, 'and it'll kick in, in due course.'

And, as usual, he turned out to be right. It was three days later when we were once again eating breakfast together that Rachael suddenly sighed, visibly relaxed and announced that Grandad was gone.

'You were aware of his presence?' I asked, fascinated, after I had welcomed her back and expressed my relief at her return.

'Oh yes, it was just like having a vast extension to my pool of personal experiences,' she said. 'I had access to everything in his memory banks and I suspect even he didn't have that. And you know what Dad? I learned a lot of surprising stuff! About what he got up to.'

Seventeen times as high as the moon

'Like what?' I leaned forward eagerly.

'No idea. I accessed it like any other memory and when Grandpa finally faded away, so did the memories. But there are traces left I think. At the edge of perception. I don't think I'll ever lose him completely.'

All this was ten years ago and I'm a grandparent myself now. Rachael lives just over in the next county where she and her family moved to be nearer the facility. Ah, I didn't mention; Rachael dropped out of her arts course, not long after my father died, and took a degree in physics and astronomy; did rather well too and is currently studying for her PhD.

Song of the spheres

Hamme sighed, leaned back in his chair and scrutinised the female on the opposite side of his desk. She was standard for her species: dark skin, mass of black hair, around forty-five k, maybe one-seventy tall. *Probably* attractive; it was hard to know. One male's mate was another one's pasta around here. Bring together the representatives of over five hundred wildly differing civilisations and you were asking for all kinds of trouble. But then, it was because there had been all kinds of trouble that they were being brought together in the first place. He sighed again, this time using his thoracic, digester orifice.

When Dwerf Thoddersman had discovered a way of forming trans-galactic wormholes for less exchange tokens than it took to purchase a pair of tail thongs, he'd opened a whole new can of, well…worms. Once every sentient creature in the galaxy was able to extend the hand of friendship to every other halfway intelligent organism, there was only one possible outcome and the ensuing war had lasted for three centuries. When peace had finally been restored, The Council had decided that the best way to maintain goodwill was to encourage a cultural exchange and that was when someone had suggested a song contest.

It had seemed like a good idea for about five Planck time units and it was during that brief interval in joined-up thinking that Hamme had been appointed to run the whole shebang. His protests regarding the impossibility of his task had fallen on deaf audio receptors.

'Cancel it?!' The Council President had retorted when Hamme had ventured to describe the logistical nightmare that the contest presented. 'Do you want to start a war?'

There being no reasonable response to that question Hamme had taken up his post and moved to The Great Sen, the giant asteroid which had been engineered to provide appropriate environmental conditions for each of the ambassadors who had attended the original peace forum. And that was as far as The Council had considered the matter.

Hamme sighed for a third time and returned his attention to Ivy League, who was, according to her biographical notes, a young woman from the human's home world, which they called, Earth. Well, they would, wouldn't they? Every crerking species called their own planet Earth...or the equivalent in their native tongue. It was the reason he'd insisted that, for the duration of the competition, they used the names given by observers from other systems. It had caused arguments, but he'd put his stride-pad down and Ivy's home was now officially, Dertangle Viz SiSi Twis and it was too late to change his mind.

'What exactly is the trouble, Miss League?' he asked, the translator's spatial sound enhancer doing a good job of centring its synthetic voice to the approximate location of his speaking organ. 'I understand you're not happy with your room share?'

'Appy? I should say I'm not 'appy. I'll 'ave you know I'm a recording artiste. I don't expect t' have t' shack up wiv some slumbag frum Gawd knows where!'

Song of the spheres

The translator was having trouble with the dialect. It was always the same; those idiots in IT never allowed for people mangling their own language – even though they'd been working on the program for two hundred years, there being constant setbacks when yet another new world was discovered and yet another new language was added to the thousands which already confronted them.

As far as he could make out, the female didn't expect to do something with something else from somewhere. Give him a clue!

'Are you talking about the other contestant Miss League? If so, I'm afraid I don't recognise the planet to which you refer. Gawdnoswere?' Anyway, what's wrong with them?'

'Wrong? They walks arand starkers, that's what's wrong!'

'Oh dear, I'm afraid you'll have to clarify that too, I can't…'

'Naked! No cloves! It ain't decent!'

Hamme called up the relevant records and studied them for a moment.

'But Miss League,' he said, 'your room companion is from Hamilton's Planet; the inhabitants there are, in your terms, analogous to giant green lobsters.'

'Yeah, well it still ain't got no cloves on!'

Hamme adopted a look of despair, realised she was unlikely to recognise that particular configuration of his secondary mandibles and opted instead, and against all common sense, for charm.

It was said that inter-species attraction was really only possible for closely related life forms. That, to take one obvious example, a lobster and a humanoid were never

Seventeen times as high as the moon

going to make it as a couple; but maybe there *were* times... Hamme had been quite taken with the dog-headed women from Cerberus II until he'd found out that they were only interested in sex once every six months. So, surely it was possible for this soft bodied, four-limbed oxygen breather to feel a degree of affection for a multi-limbed, nitrogen imbiber with a half exoskeleton? He'd give it a go.

'Ivy. You don't mind if I call you Ivy, do you? Ivy, I quite understand your position, really I do. Some of us are more sensitive than others, aren't we? You'd be amazed what certain alien beings are prepared to put up with. Honestly! And the problems they cause me!

'Do you know only yesterday I had a representative of the Harp People from Shhqrsteen Olvo in this office. And do you know what they wanted? They wanted me to transfer them from 'Choirs' to the 'Family Group' category because they said it was quite normal for their females to give birth to forty offspring! Incidentally, they're curious characters. They sing by letting the wind blow through the exposed tendons in their pseudo feet and flexing the muscles to modulate the sound. Apparently, on their own planet, the wind always blows from east to west – or maybe it's west to east – and they spend all their life facing in one direction, which is why they've evolved a wedge-shaped body.'

He paused, aware that he was talking too much. He waited for a response but none came. Unexpectedly, Ivy seemed to be enthralled with his narrative. Hesitantly, he continued.

'You've no idea how difficult this job is, Ivy. I've got contestants from gas giants who are floating bladders and whose song is a giant fart you can hear all over the

Song of the spheres

planet!' He stopped again, recalling rather belatedly that flatulence wasn't a subject that all species found amusing. And for a moment it seemed that Ivy's might be just one such as she was making an odd noise in her throat, which on his own world would, historically, have preceded ritual disembowelling. He tapped urgently at his information bulb and learned, delightfully, that the sound was a "giggle", a response indicating an engaged amusement. Encouraged, he ploughed on.

'You know, there are mineral-based entities here whose performances are expected to last centuries?' It was true, although immaterial. In fact, The Great Sen was travelling at near light speed, which meant that most of the contestants with short life-spans would find everyone they knew dead, by the time the results were announced and they returned home. Hamme wasn't convinced that everyone aboard had understood the briefing and so he kept quiet on that particular aspect of the journey.

'Look, Ivy, do you fancy a mug of frithtangle?' He consulted his bulb, tried again. 'A coffee? Tea?'

'Yeah, why not, eh? 'Ere, you one uh the judges? P'rhaps I kin give yer arm a twist, watta y'fink?' and she giggled again. Hamme closed all five eyes and shivered right down to his lower fidgedringer.

The canteen lounge was crowded despite being limited to category 'C' visitors. A group of Thossles from The Queem Particulate was in indirect conversation with two Shape-Shifters from Prong's Tressle. Hamme frowned. He'd thought the Shifters had left for home after been disqualified during the early heats. Having seemingly won their way through to the competition

Seventeen times as high as the moon

proper, the Shifters when asked to reprise their successful song had been forced to admit that they were physically unable to sing and had merely assumed the body shapes of another duo whom they had eaten as part of the previous evening's supper.

Food. Well, that was a whole new disaster waiting to happen. Half the contestants were food for the other half. Many had been forced to bring their supplies with them. Where, for instance, could you get Grufus dung, the only comestible acceptable to the people of Vanity 15? Well, only on Vanity 15, that was where. You just had to be so cautious. Pot plants could turn out to be contestants. Last week, a puddle licked up by a pet poodlehooch from Zachron Darside had proved to be one third of a singing group from the water world of Benni. A couple of months ago, workmen clearing the site had felled six of the entrants from Onglethrop IV who had taken root shortly after their arrival. There were actions pending in dozens of cases and at least one declaration of war had needed to be hurriedly suppressed using a diplomatic tactic which, Hamme suspected, involved an accident with an open airlock.

He carefully repositioned a fruit creature from Fipp Zin Bap Bap which had fallen asleep dangerously near to the dessert trolley and indicated for Ivy to sit down.

'What are you singing,' he asked, as they waited for the serverbot to reach their table. 'Something traditional? New wave?' Actually, he had no idea whether either of those terms had relevance on Dertangle Viz SiSi Twis/Earth and was just content to make conversation and enjoy the human's company.

Song of the spheres

'Betcha Betcha Doobie Dah' replied Ivy. At least, he assumed it was a reply and not the name of the planet from which she had culled her musical offering.

'Sounds nice,' he lied, with what he hoped might be a smile. 'The galaxy's full of music – quite literally. Your recordings for instance. If they've been broadcast, and I bet they have!...' he attempted a wink, closed an external nasal spiracle instead and went on, '...they'll travel off into space forever on waves of sound. It's a kind of immortality, isn't it?'

Ivy fluttered her eyelids in what might have been a response. ''Ere, I do like the way you talk,' she said, ''though I don't know what yer on abhat 'alf the time.'

'Radio waves,' elucidated Hamme, 'they keep on rolling across the ether. There are some guys here playing stuff they picked up from a civilisation on the other side the galaxy! Took millions of years to reach them apparently. There's an agent on The Great Sen suing them for posthumous royalties on behalf of the composers' descendants. But just think of it Ivy: your songs, still echoing around space all that time after you sing them!'

This time she laughed, which intriguingly for both parties was a Fringalongan invitation to engage in sex. Fringalonga was the name given by the Throssles to the planet on which Hamme had pupated and he took Ivy's action as a final confirmation of the interest she had first expressed when she had coquettishly suggested that she might 'twist his arm'; although where on anybody's Earth she might have heard that particular euphemism was an open question.

Seventeen times as high as the moon

Primary encounter

'So, these are your famous Martians.' Annie leaned forward and peered down into the glass dome, which occupied a central position on the low worktop. It was small, no more than half a metre wide, and from its top a number of cables and flexible tubes ran up to a conduit above her head. On the dome's floor, a collection of irregularly shaped stones was strewn, apparently at random, across a layer of dusty, red sand over which tiny forms, which echoed the shape of the enclosing hemisphere, crawled with infinite slowness.

'They're not exactly "little green men", are they?' She looked up at the white-coated figure across the table and grinned, lopsidedly.

'They're not exactly *mine*, either,' responded Professor Andy Colshaugh, 'just my responsibility, which is more than enough, I assure you... and I'm sorry that you find our very first extra-terrestrial visitors so unprepossessing.'

'Visitors?' Annie adopted an expression of mock indignation. 'Scooped up by a foraging lander and transported however many million miles it is before being locked up in your lab. Sounds more like kidnap to me. If you're not careful you'll have their friends' tripods laying waste the Earth in retaliation!'

'At three mills diameter and with no appendages of any sort, I think they might have trouble operating the controls...and it's around one hundred and forty million, on average.'

'What is?'

Seventeen times as high as the moon

'The distance between the two planets; varies quite a bit; can be as much as two hundred and forty-nine million or as close as just thirty-four.'

'Thirty-four million miles is still a long way from home.'

'I don't think they'll be complaining. They may have no recognisable nervous system, leave alone a rudimentary brain,' the professor frowned suddenly, 'in fact, to be honest, I'm a long way from working out what make them tick.'

Annie leaned back towards the dome and cocked her head to one side. 'Can't hear a thing,' she said, shaking her blonde bob in a way that she knew Andy found irresistible.

'They probably need winding!' He stepped round the table and kissed her impulsively on the lips.

***

She had not been to the laboratory for several weeks. Her own schedule had kept her busy and during their irregular night time telephone calls Andy had made it clear that international clamour for news of the aliens had placed him under immense pressure.

'I can't help thinking sometimes,' he told her one evening, 'that it would have been easier if that damned probe had loaded nothing more exciting than sand into its hopper. And after all, what were the chances, eh? The Americans have had a dozen vehicles combing the Martian surface for decades – *and* the Chinese. Who the hell would have foreseen that the ESA would hit pay-dirt with their very first expedition, and with a British-built soil sampler on board? Rule Britannia!

Primary encounters

And now the world's media are expecting daily bulletins on our Martian chums. It's like a bloody royal birth! - and I'm the midwife.'

'It's compensation,' Annie told him, 'for the fact that the Martians turned out to be slugs with an appetite for carbon dioxide. People are disappointed. Oh, we all understood that there wouldn't be intelligent life on The Red Planet but having it confirmed, finally killed the dream. It's like discovering that Santa Claus doesn't exist. All those stories. Remember Edgar Rice Burroughs's Barsoom?'

'Ah yes, the scantily clad princesses.'

'Quite. And H G Wells and Ray Bradbury...'

'Weren't Wells' Martians wiped out by human pathogens?'

'That's right, and so were Bradbury's, more or less. The poor old Martians don't benefit much from contact with Earth.'

'That'll teach 'em to invade us! Anyway, how come you know all this stuff?'

'I'm a literary agent, remember? The clue's in the title. And by the way, in Bradbury's stories, *we* colonise Mars and take the disease with us. Look, the point is that we've grown so used to the idea of an intelligent race on Mars that, however irrational it might be, we're disappointed to discover they're not there. So now, we want whatever we can get.'

Andy grunted his acceptance of the argument. 'Personally, I'd *welcome* creatures with a higher IQ. If the real aliens were able to speak for themselves I wouldn't have to play nursemaid twenty-four seven. But there *are* compensations, you're right. I don't know about the little men from Mars - the guys over at

Seventeen times as high as the moon

NASA were the ones who were green when they heard we'd found life forms among the returning samples. Chuck Peters was apoplectic when I told him the size of the UK contribution. "Holy shit!" he said. "We pumped billions into our Mars programme and you Limey bastards struck lucky first time, and *that* was only because you fouled up your trajectories and landed in the wrong place!"

'Blame the French, I told him, 'they were the ones in charge of the flight operation. Once the payload was on board we were just spectators until after the landing.'

'Still, Mr Peters is right, I suppose. You did strike lucky.'

'Uh! It was damn nearly a total disaster! The lander missed the target by three thousand kilometres and broke through the crust on impact. What *was* lucky was that the whole expedition wasn't written off within seconds of our arrival.'

'But under the crust...'

'Were my little charges, yeah. The first extra-terrestrial life-forms encountered by mankind in its quest to boldly go where no man has gone before – oops, sorry, to go boldly, where no man has gone before.'

Annie laughed. 'To infinitive and beyond! Pleased to see that my influence has rubbed off on the senior scientist! And seriously, it is quite an accolade to be the man entrusted with their care.'

'Yeah, yeah, second-hand immortality: my name as a footnote in the pages of history...'

'Don't be so dismissive of your contribution. There isn't a scientist on the planet who wouldn't give his eyeteeth for just a glimpse of those critters. They've

Primary encounters

come to you because you're the Earth's leading exobiologist, remember that.'

'I'm the Earth's ONLY exobiologist, whose interest isn't entirely theoretical! So, yeah, that does make me a leader in my field if only by default. Look, Annie, you've got me wrong. I'm not trying to decry the significance of the event I promise you. What's bugging me is the need to communicate every last detail of my research to any Tom, Dick or Harry who attends those bloody daily press conferences. I've told the PR guys, there won't *be* any research if I spend my whole day answering damn fool questions from Hello Magazine and Caged Birds Weekly!'

'You mean, Scientific American and Nature, I suppose.'

'Yeah, well... under the Martian crust, when those magnificent Frenchmen's flying machine finally came to rest, we found a thin film of salty brine and ultimately, our friends the Martians; but only after we'd vacuum-packed our deep-soil samples and returned them to Earth for analysis. That's when things went haywire.'

'Haywire? How, haywire?'

'Because there shouldn't have been anything living, that near the planetary surface, that's how. For a half-dozen reasons.'

'Give me one.'

'Radiation. Mar's has had no magnetic field for several billion years. All that cosmic and solar radiation should have scoured the place clean. No cell structure we know of could survive that kind of onslaught.'

Seventeen times as high as the moon

'And what kind of cell structure have the Martians got?'

'Search me! No one's going to authorise a biopsy, leave alone an autopsy, on anything so precious. Maybe if one of them dies…if I can tell that it's died that is. Right now, I'm not able to do much more than observe and speculate.'

'Poor love. You didn't tell me all this when I visited your lab.'

'No, well I was distracted, remember?'

Annie giggled. 'Oh, yes,' she whispered, 'I remember!'

***

'Am I under arrest?'

'Hardly. You're not shackled to the chair, are you?'

'No, but I was frogmarched down here under armed guard!'

'Escorted to the canteen and offered a cup of tea was how I heard it.'

'He had a gun.'

'Yes, well, security's been stepped up since the protest.'

'Mmm, I heard on the news that you had a spot of bother; what happened?'

'A bunch of idiot students tried to liberate our Martian visitors.'

'Hostages.'

'Eh?'

Hostages, not visitors; I told you there'd be consequences if you kidnapped a group of foreign nationals.'

Primary encounters

'It's not funny, Annie.' Andy turned from where he had been standing in the open doorway and nodded at the returning security guard who was carrying a drinks carton in each hand.

'Thanks so much Ben, I'll take them from here; and Miss Cavendish offers her profound apologies for ignoring security protocols.'

'S'not a problem Professor, but as you know, after last week's little debacle we dumped the old security tags. If the young lady would call into the office later, I'll organise an iris scan and get her onto the system.' He looked over Andy's shoulder and flashed a grin. 'I don't think we need do a full background check under the circumstances, Miss.'

'What circumstances would those be?' asked Annie as the guard retreated along the corridor and Andy set the drinks down on the table and pulled up a chair.

Andy sighed and ran a hand through his hair. 'To be frank, there aren't any; and Ben's bending the rules giving you clearance just on my say so.'

'Oh dear, you *are* serious and I really am sorry I just waltzed through reception and set off the alarms. Obviously, things have been more complicated than the press have reported. They're just saying there was an incident at the facility. So, what *did* happen?'

'A bunch of young activists with an agenda: that's what happened. They broke in and managed to smash up some of the equipment before Ben and his boys took control.

'What sort of agenda? I take it from your reaction to my annoying quip that they weren't really alien liberationists.'

Seventeen times as high as the moon

'Sorry if I snapped, it's been a difficult few days; and no, they weren't trying to free the Martians, their objection was on behalf of their starving fellow humans. Money that could be better spent; and who's to say they aren't right? Do you know what this whole exercise has cost so far, including our involvement in the expedition?'

'Those arguments seldom make sense and you know it. For heaven's sake Andy, those are Martians you've got in there. I think most people are too excited about that to think of the bill.' She paused, studying his face. 'But there's more, isn't there. You're too involved to be getting depressed about the allocation of funds; something else is keeping you awake at night. Am I right?'

'They detached the life support - when they broke in. For over an hour, the creatures were exposed to Earth atmosphere.'

'And…'

Andy shrugged. 'I'm still assessing the effect.'

'But it didn't kill them?'

'That's the question everyone from the Director down wants answered and the honest truth is…I don't know.' Andy thrust his chair back from the table and leaned forward, elbows on knees, hands clasped in a parody of prayer. 'The Earth's leading exobiologist – your words, not mine remember – and I can't tell you if the damn things are dead or alive!'

'They were crawling around when I saw them, surely that's a clue.'

'Haven't moved a muscle since the protest – if they've got muscles, which is doubtful. But there was one very odd thing when I got to them, after the lab crew had repaired the breach in the environmental dome: they were completely immobile but they'd formed themselves into a regular pattern on the dome floor. I've got to assume that was after the breach – they'd never shown any tendency to group response before – and so they didn't die immediately, even if they're dead now. Leaving the question, why did they respond in that way? Was it some kind of defence mechanism and if so, was it effective? At the moment we're keeping them under twenty-four-hour surveillance but if they remain inactive much longer, we'll have to make assumptions about their probable demise and think about reaching for the scalpel.'

'Which, in a way, is just what you wanted, isn't it?'

'Well, I can't deny relishing the opportunity to examine one of the little critters but I wasn't expecting to do it at the expense of all its mates.'

Annie placed the empty cups one in the other and stood.

'I was wondering about that,' she said, walking round to Andy's side of the table and taking his hands in hers, 'whether they really have mates, I mean. Has there been any sign of them pairing up?'

He smiled up at her, despite his mood. 'None that I've seen,' he replied. 'Of course, they may be completely asexual.'

'Poor things, said Annie, bending and kissing him gently on the mouth.

***

'I saw the press release: "Martians alive and well!" So, you don't get to wield the knife after all. Disappointed?'

Seventeen times as high as the moon

Andy pivoted a hand in a gesture intended to convey his ambivalence. One of the fingers was heavily strapped.

'Don't tell me they bit you?' Her concern was clear despite her usual bantering tone. 'Must be that whiff of oxygen they got the other day; it's given them a taste for red meat!'

'As a matter of fact, you're right on two scores.' Andy grinned, closed the door to his office behind her and, clearing a chair of files and loose documents, indicated for her to sit.

'The morning after I saw you last they were still in the same pattern; no sign of life. So, as agreed by those on high, I decided to choose a specimen and give it the once over, top to toe,' he reached across and placed a finger on her lips – 'no, I'm sure they haven't, don't interrupt the professor when he's lecturing. Anyway, as soon as I made contact, the whole collection were in motion. The nearest few made it to my hand and, before I pulled away, one of them had scissored its way into my finger! So, yes, I did get bitten and yes, I theorise that it was the high oxygen levels that changed their behaviour. I don't know about the red meat, you'll have to make do with two out of three.'

'But is it OK?' she indicated the bandaged digit. 'Could you be infected?'

'Probably not in the manner you're thinking of but the doc took blood samples for analysis and the results are…interesting.'

'Interesting? I'm not sure I like "interesting".'

'Annie, listen.' He had taken a seat on the edge of his desk facing her chair and now he leaned down and fixed

Primary encounters

her look of concern with eyes which sparkled with excitement.

'I don't believe the organisms up in my lab are Martians at all.'

'Not Martians? But they did come from the planet between here and Saturn, didn't they? Popularly known as Mars, I believe.'

'Oh, that's where they came from all right and it's where they were created too.'

'Created?'

'By the real Martians: a genuine, sentient race who evolved on The Red Planet and who faced extinction when their atmosphere began to be stripped away by the solar wind.'

'Ye gods! You mean it, don't you? John Carter and Dejah Thoris!'

'Not quite that, no; but some sort of civilisation certainly. One capable of quite advanced technology even if in limited areas of activity.'

'Would there have been time for them to evolve? Hasn't Mars been barren for millions of years?'

'There's evidence that Mars had an oxygen rich atmosphere over four billion years ago. That's one-and-a-half billion years before Earth's own atmospheric oxygen formed; and maybe their rate of development was much faster than ours.'

'But what's led you to this idea?' Annie looked anxious now, studying his face for signs of stress.

'That blood test. Something curious showed up in the DNA. Have you heard of Leonard Adleman?'

'I don't think so, no.'

'Way back in 1994 he proposed that DNA strands could be used for computation. DNA is a coding

Seventeen times as high as the moon

system for the human body and he saw how that might make it ideal for data processing. I think that maybe, when that thing bit me, it was sampling my own DNA. Because, that's what they are Annie, those creatures: components of an organic computer system!'

This time Annie didn't respond, she merely continued to study Andy's face, waiting for him to complete his revelations.

'Imagine,' he continued, when he saw she was expecting more, 'those original Martians; because of the degradation of the atmosphere they knew they were doomed and, as I suggested, their levels of technical ability didn't offer an escape from their planet. But maybe their skills lay elsewhere: in physiology, in gene manipulation and so that's where they put all their effort at finding a plan for survival. They created those bugs upstairs. Simple molecular components which, when linked together formed a processor capable of carrying all the knowledge of their civilisation; and they did it by using their DNA to store data!'

By now Andy's face was shining with anticipation and wonder.

'Annie, that ship only brought back a few dozen organisms. There may be hundreds of thousands surviving under the crust of the planet; maybe millions! But if I'm right, we only need one. It's been calculated that a pound of DNA has the capacity to store more data than all the electronic computers ever built. Everything the Martians wanted to tell us could be encoded in the DNA of a single creature. The rest are just back up. Like acorns on a tree; most of them are wasted; the tree produces thousands to ensure that at least one makes it through to germination. And just one of the Martians'

Primary encounters

bugs holds everything they wanted us to know. All it needs is the stimulation of oxygen. The Martians knew that they were losing their own supply so they must have anticipated that one day we would arrive and learn to trigger their creations into life.'

'But surely, at the time, life would barely have begun to evolve on the Earth? Could they really have been so far-seeing?'

'If they were, it makes me shiver with anticipation as to what we may be able to learn.'

'There's just one thing I don't understand.' Annie had left the chair and was circling the office, as she grappled with the concept of a vanished race of super intelligent beings and their compulsion to save what they had learned for whoever might come after them. 'How do we access this stuff? It may be built into the DNA of a million tiny entities but where's the output socket? How do we get at it?'

Andy looked suddenly sober. The wonder still showed in his eyes but a new emotion had replaced the anticipation, one revealed by the tension in his body and the tightly clenched fists. In a moment of realisation Annie saw that it was trepidation: a fear of what he was about to tell her.

'It's that "interesting" blood test, isn't it?'

He nodded.

'A string of mutated genes. They're already causing some sort of rewrite in my own DNA. We assume that whatever's encoded within them will make itself clear in some way we don't yet understand.'

'I think I might,' said Annie coming to stand so close to him that he could see little more than her eyes and a frame of unfocussed blonde hair. 'You're a scientist.

Seventeen times as high as the moon

You think in terms of what you can learn about the world; how the universe works; where the cogs fit together. It's pure research just for the joy of knowing. But that's not how everyone thinks. Some of us only see benefit in knowledge if it can be used to fulfil a purpose. And I think that's how the Martian's would have felt when they realised their planet was doomed. Their first thought wouldn't have been how they could leave a doubtful legacy for some imaginary future space-farer, it would have been how they could provide for their own immortality. What they would have built into those creatures' DNA is their own blueprint.'

Andy stared back into her unblinking eyes

'But how…'

'Andy, you're so impractical. I would have thought that the method was obvious. Do you think that our children will be green?'

Printed in Great Britain
by Amazon